TRANS FORMERS™

THE NOVEL

A Novelization by S. G. Wilkens

Based on the Screenplay by

Roberto Orci & Alex Kurtzman from a

Story by Roberto Orci &

Alex Kurtzman and John Rogers

HarperCollins *Children's Books*

Transformers: The Novel

First published by HarperCollins Children's Books in 2007

HarperCollins Children's Books is a division of HarperCollins Publishers Ltd.

1 2 3 4 5 6 7 8 9 10

978-000-725102-5

0-00-725102-5

The HarperCollins website address is: www.harpercollinschildrensbooks.co.uk

Printed and bound in Spain

TRANSFORMERS™

TRANSFORMERS™

THE NOVEL

PROLOGUE

One million years before the dawn of man, a distant planet was destroyed by the ravages of war. The war was between those who worshipped chaos and those who followed freedom.

The inhabitants of this planet battled for control of the supreme power, the Allspark, the only remaining source of their life force, which had created their race. The fight dragged on until the world was awash in death, until the ground swallowed whole their once-mighty cities, and until both sides lost the Allspark forever to the limitless stars.

The Allspark hurtled into space . . . but then, its course was altered. It drifted toward a small, curious planet. Earth.

Many freedom fighters searched for the Allspark, hoping they could find it before the dark legions did. But they were already too late.

Captain Archibald Witwicky watched as his men chopped away at the ice. "Put your backs into it," he cried, "or we'll be chopping our way back to the States!" His ship, the *Discovery*, had snagged on an iceberg, which had put him behind schedule for his great Arctic voyage of 1897. He had a lot of territory to explore and precious little time.

He tapped some ice off his glasses as the huskies began to bark and pull on their leashes. Suddenly, the ropes snapped, and the dogs bolted out into the snow. "There's something out there," said the captain's first mate.

Captain Witwicky grabbed his rifle and lantern. "Both of you." He pointed to two of his crewmen. "Come with me."

They could barely see the outlines of the dogs' bodies as they sped across the ice. Suddenly, the huskies stopped, made a few small whimpers, and started digging at the snow.

"Whatever it is, it's below the ice," one of the captain's men whispered.

"But nothing could be alive below the ice," the captain reminded him.

All at once, the ground split. A huge hole formed, sucking down the surrounding ice, snow, and one of the dogs. Captain Witwicky tried to pull the dog to safety, but instead, she dragged him thirty feet down into the hole.

They landed with a thud. Dazed but not hurt, the captain opened his eyes. It was very cold and dark down there. The lantern's flickering light spilled shadows across the pale blue, frozen walls. "I'm okay, lads!" he called up the hole.

The captain turned around, and his mouth fell open. An enormous . . . thing . . . was just inches away. It seemed to be a face, its huge jaws hanging open, seemingly paralyzed in a silent scream. As the captain's eyes adjusted, he saw there was a gigantic body below, crystallized in the ice. It had the shape of a man—it had a head, a torso, arms, and legs.

Only this body wasn't made of flesh; it seemed to be made of metal. The captain squinted through his glasses. Was this a machine? A strange vehicle of some sort? He wiped ice off the body to examine the badge emblazoned across the giant's chest. It had five sides, with pointy top edges and a design in the center. The symbol looked like a mask.

He used his pickax to chop away at the ice around the Ice Man's head and torso, growing more and more excited. This was an explorer's dream: A discovery like this would most definitely put him up there with the greats. Pizarro. Cortés. Columbus!

When his ax hit a certain spot on the Ice Man's chest, however, a horrible, deafening screech let out. Then, a bright beam shot from the monster, flooding the cave with hot, white light. The captain covered his eyes and fell to the ground, gasping. For a few seconds, he could see nothing but millions of strange symbols. The symbols seemed to link together, like a code.

"Captain?" his men called. "Captain?"

All at once, the screeching sound stopped, and the light blinked out. Eager to see what had happened, the captain fumbled for his glasses—the force of the beam had knocked them off his face. As he groped to find them, he realized he couldn't see the ground. He couldn't see anything. He was blind!

When his crewmen finally dug him out, the captain was frostbitten, starved, and near-dead. But he wouldn't stop talking about the man he had seen down in the ice cave, an enormous Ice Man who had shot lights through his eyes and had a strange, masklike symbol on his chest. However, everyone thought the ordeal had affected his mind, and no one listened to him.

They should have.

Sergeant William Lennox looked out the window of the CV-22 air force plane as it flew over a Qatar desert. He and his men of the army's 5th Special Forces Security team had just completed a tough mission and were finally returning to base. He turned to the soldier beside him, Army Chief Warrant Officer John Figueroa. "Tell me the first thing you're going to do when you get home."

"Surfboard on the roof, headed for turquoise water," Figueroa—or Fig, as everyone called him—answered in his Louisianan Cajun drawl.

"I hear that," Lennox said. Their tour in the desert was scheduled to last another sixteen months, but everyone was already thinking about home.

"When I get back, I'm gonna have me a perfect day," Fig went on. "One of those days where everything just goes right." He turned to his buddy. "How 'bout you, Lennox? What's your perfect day?"

Lennox stared at his worn boots. "Holding my

little girl for the first time."

Their helicopter approached the base, the Special Operations Command Center (SOCCENT). Lennox felt suddenly upbeat; now that their mission was over, things might calm down for a while. Maybe he'd even have time to call his wife, Sarah, and hear the first coos of his baby daughter, Annabelle, who had been born just two weeks after he'd left. That would be perfect enough for him, at least for right now.

Inside the SOCCENT base watchtower, however, something was wrong. "There's an inbound unidentified infiltrator ten miles out," the watch sergeant warned his commander, pointing to a blinking red light on his radar screen.

The commander pushed the sergeant aside, stared at the radar, and calmly took the radio microphone. "You're in restricted U.S. military airspace," he called to the unknown plane. "Identify yourself and proceed east out of the area."

There was no response. The commander furrowed his brow. So that was how it was going to be. He radioed for the two scout planes that circled the base at all times. "Raptors One and Two. Proceed to

7

intercept the unidentified aircraft."

Raptor One banked hard to tail the stranger. The pilot's eyes widened as he realized it was a Special Ops Command helicopter. The thing was massive . . . and unusual for these parts.

"Unidentified aircraft," Raptor One radioed to the strange chopper, "we'll escort you to the U.S. SOCCENT air base—if you don't comply, we'll use deadly force."

Although the chopper didn't identify itself, it did start to make its way for the ground. The Raptor pilot followed it closely, calling the watchtower again. "It's coming down," the pilot said. "Tail ID is 4500X-ray."

Moments later, the op-center technicians had a result on the tail ID. "You're not going to believe this," the techie said to the watch commander, "but 4500X was shot down three months ago. In Afghanistan."

The commander frowned. Shot down? "Gotta be a mistake."

The helicopter settled slowly to the earth in a storm of dust. Armed Humvees circled it.

"Unidentified aircraft, shut down and step out now," the watch commander shouted through the loudspeaker. He took out his binoculars and zoomed in on the strange chopper's cockpit. The pilot, a man with a mustache, sat motionless. When the Humvee soldiers aimed their weapons at the craft, the pilot didn't even flinch.

Then, the commander saw something through his binoculars that nearly made his heart stop. The pilot began to shimmer and short out, like a fuzzy television image. Within seconds, he had disintegrated into thin air.

Lennox and his men had just stepped onto the tarmac when the strange chopper came down beside them. The Humvee soldiers told them to get back and take cover. They, too, saw the mustached pilot shimmer and disappear. And then, something even stranger happened. The chopper started to transform.

First, its rotors retracted. Its steel frame peeled back, split apart, and stacked on top of itself, growing taller. The cockpit and wheels became its feet, the interior and engine formed its torso, and the fuselage stripped away to reveal a head and two massive arms. On its chest was an emblem in the shape of a pentagon, with pointy top edges and a design in the center. It looked like a mask.

Lennox put his hand over his mouth. The chopper had completely transformed into a *giant* armored man. It towered over the rest of the vehicles on the base.

The creature sprang to life, shooting a round of bright, powerful beams at the ground, and disintegrating a row of cargo planes. It stepped on an empty airplane hangar and swiped at the barracks. The men in the Humvees tried shooting at it, but the bullets bounced right off the thing's armor.

When the mechanoid grabbed a thick, tightly wrapped cord of high-wire cables that hung above the barracks, everyone in the watchtower panicked—those cables connected all the electronics and computers of the entire base! The wires came spookily alive, twisting and curling in the air like hypnotized snakes. The machine squeezed them tightly and emitted a high-intensity shriek.

Up in the tower, an ominous message flickered on the watch commander's monitor: FILE UPLOADING: PROJECT ICE MAN: ABOVE TOP SECRET: SECTOR SEVEN ACCESS ONLY.

It was hacking their files.

"Cut the hard lines! Cut the hard lines!" the watch commander screamed.

The airman ripped an ax from the wall and chopped away at the mainframe controls. Soon, all the computer monitors went dark, and the cables fizzled and slumped in the robot's hands.

Enraged, the robot glared at the watchtower. A bright red warning light on its chest began to blink. In seconds, a white-hot laser shot from the creature's arm, incinerating another row of planes.

Lennox and his team bolted for cover. The only way to safety, though, was through the giant steel legs. They ducked and weaved, the monster's gargantuan feet nearly flattening them. Fig stumbled over shrapnel and started to roll. He landed hard on the ground, right under the monster. Although he knew it was risky, Fig pulled out his thermal imager and took a quick snap of the monster's complicated underbelly.

"No!" Lennox cried, waving Fig away. "It senses your imager!"

The robot gave Fig an ominous stare. The red warning light on its chest started to blink again. Fig scrambled to safety as huge fireballs swept across the ground. Thinking fast, he unhooked his high-heat laser launcher and blindly fired at the thing, just to distract it. Beams zoomed through the air, and one of them hit the monster right in the chest. The monster staggered backward, screaming in pain. Its limbs trembled, and it fell with a shudder. When the dust cleared, Lennox and the others saw that the thing lay motionless on its back.

"Let's get out of here!" Lennox cried. And they did.

Sam Witwicky sat in the back of history class, staring at Mikaela Banes, the most beautiful girl at Tranquility High. They would make such a good couple. *So what if she's an inch taller than me? Why does she have to go out with that jerk, Trent DeMarco?*

"'Kay, Sam, you're up," Mr. Hosney, the teacher, called.

Seriously, what does Trent have that I don't? Besides playing on the football team and owning a cool car. . . .

"Dude." Sam's best friend, Miles, snapped his fingers in front of Sam's face. "Earth. Now."

Sam jumped, grabbed his backpack, and walked to the front of the room. Kids began to giggle and throw wadded-up pieces of paper at his back.

"Um, so, for my family genealogy report, I picked my great-great-grandfather, Captain Archibald Witwicky, one of the first guys to ever make it to the Arctic Circle," Sam started. As he opened his backpack, he felt something squishy land in his hair. He peeled it off slowly and squinted. It was a red gummy worm. "Ah, cherry. My favorite."

With as much dignity as he could muster, he laid out his great-great-grandfather's artifacts on the table. A compass . . . a sextant . . . and an old-fashioned pair of glasses.

"So, like, here are some ancient navigational tools," he started, holding each up. The class looked bored. "And I'm selling this stuff on the Internet to make money for my car fund. They make really cool Christmas gifts, available at a low, low price . . ."

"Sam . . . ," Mr. Hosney interrupted.

Sam shifted back to the report. "Right, anyway, I guess years of hypothermia froze my great-great-grandpa's brain, and he ended up going blind and crazy in a sanitarium. All he did was draw these weird symbols and babble about a giant ice man."

He held up a newspaper clipping from 1897. The headline read, ARCTIC ADVENTURER ALLEGES ICE MAN FOUND! Beneath it was a picture of Captain

Witwicky, holding up crude sketches of the mask symbol he had seen on the Ice Man's chest.

Sam opened his mouth to continue, but the bell rang. As students filed out, Mr. Hosney glared at him. "Saved by the bell," he deadpanned.

"So . . . what's my grade?" Sam asked.

"A solid B minus."

"B minus? What about all the visual aids?"

Mr. Hosney shrugged. "Wasn't really feeling it."

"No, you don't get it," Sam explained desperately. "My dad said last year that when I turned sixteen, if I saved two thousand bucks and got three As, he'd help me buy half a car. I have all the money saved, and two As . . . so I need at least an A minus."

But Mr. Hosney looked unconvinced.

"Please," Sam said, practically throwing himself at his teacher's feet. "My future—my freedom—my *manhood*—is in your merciful hands."

Mr. Hosney heaved a sigh. Sam knew he was going to say yes.

After school, Sam giddily sat beside his father as they cruised Tranquility's Auto Row. He couldn't wait to pick out his new car! But his face fell when his father pulled into a used-car lot called Bolivia's Auto Resale.

"Here?" Sam cried. "No, no, no, no, Dad. These cars say to girls, 'Run, run *away* from this spaz.'"

His father parked and got out. "I think they say you're the guy who knows the value of a hard-earned buck, kiddo. No sacrifice, no victory."

Sam sighed. Dad *always* said that.

A shifty-looking man in a shiny blue suit ran out of the used-car lot's office. "Gentlemen, hiya," he said, extending his hand. "Bobby Bolivia, at your service."

"My son's buying his first car," Sam's father explained.

Bobby grinned lopsidedly at Sam. "I've been doing this a long time, kid, and, see, the drivers don't pick their cars, no sir. The cars pick their driver. It's a mystical bond between man and machine."

Sam walked up and down the rows of cars, his hopes dissolving fast. Each car was uglier and more beat up than the next. He hesitated at a beat-up yellow Camaro. Sam traced his finger along the Camaro's cheaply affixed black racing stripes. At least this one wasn't a minivan.

Bobby rushed over and stared confusedly at the Camaro. "Wait. Where'd this come from?" He looked over his shoulder toward his ramshackle office. "Manny!" he screamed. "What the heck's this?"

Sam opened the Camaro's door. It actually had an operational eight-track player. Then, a glint of light caught his eye. A strange symbol was emblazoned on the steering wheel. It reminded him of the kooky mask his great-great-grandpa Captain Witwicky drew when he was in the loony bin.

"How much?" Mr. Witwicky asked Bobby.

Bobby scratched his head. "Uh . . . five grand."

"We're not going above four."

Bobby glowered. "Kid, hands off the car."

"But you said the cars pick the drivers," Sam complained.

"Well, sometimes they choose one that's outta their price range." Bobby pointed to a beater two rows over. "Now, this one here's beautiful . . ."

The Camaro's horn suddenly blared. The noise was so loud, everyone jumped, and all of the windows in every other car on the lot shattered. Sam jumped back as glass splintered onto the pavement. "What was *that*?" he cried.

"Oh, nooo!" Bobby screamed. Glass continued to spill all over the concrete, breaking off in dangerous shards. "Manny! Get out here!"

Mr. Witwicky grabbed Sam's hand and led him back to their car. "Wait!" Bobby chased after them. "Okay, it's your lucky day! Because of the glitches, you can have the Camaro for four thousand."

Sam looked at his Dad. "Please?" Mr. Witwicky looked torn, but finally nodded.

"Yes!" Sam cried.

RAND CORPORATION HEADQUARTERS,
WASHINGTON, D.C.

maggie Marconi couldn't believe her bad luck. This morning, she'd had to hide from her landlord because her rent was overdue, which made her too late to catch the train, meaning she had to grab a cab . . . which proceeded to get stuck in traffic for forty-five minutes. Of all the days for things to go wrong: Her very first code encryption brief for her new employer, the Rand Corporation, was due at four P.M. sharp. Maggie didn't want to make a bad first impression—or worse, get fired, which was exactly what had happened at her last job.

As she frantically skidded into the Rand complex, two agents in mirrored sunglasses tapped her on the shoulder. "Maggie Marconi?" One of them flashed his Secret Service badge. "We need you to come with us." He took her arm.

Maggie's heart pounded. *Uh-oh. What did I do?* She and her code-cracking colleague, Glen

Whitman, sometimes dabbled in stuff they shouldn't—like hacking into the traffic grid to make all the stoplights on a particularly busy street go green. "Hey, I have a right to know where I'm going!" she cried.

"You'll see shortly," the second agent said, nudging her out the double doors. A chopper sat on Rand's front lawn. To Maggie's utter surprise, they got in and began to fly to the Pentagon.

Once there, they rushed down a series of hallways to a set of closed double doors. A sergeant stopped Maggie. "Miss, you need to sign this classified nondisclosure agreement."

Maggie's hand shook as she signed her name. What was she doing here? This would get her fired from Rand for sure. Next, they led her into a room that was already full of people. Maggie sat in a chair near the door, next to a young guy who looked as confused as she was.

Another door opened, and a tall, sturdily built man entered. Immediately, everyone stood. The guy to Maggie's left went pale. "That's John Keller, the Secretary of Defense," he murmured, even though Maggie—and everyone else—was already perfectly aware of who John Keller was.

"Sit," John Keller said, and everyone did. "Obviously, you're wondering why you're here. These are the facts: At oh-nine-hundred local time yesterday, the SOCCENT base in Qatar was attacked. There were no survivors."

Everyone gasped.

Keller silenced them. "The objective of the attack was to hack our military network—we aren't sure exactly what they were after, but we do know they were cut off during the assault. We think they'll try again. No one's claimed responsibility, and our only lead is this signal."

A noise screeched through the speakers. It was the sound the mechanical beast made when squeezing the wires at the Qatar base—it was like fingernails scraping down a chalkboard.

"That's what hacked our network," Keller said, when the signal stopped. "We're trying to analyze it to find out who did this, but we need your help. You've all shown considerable ability in the area of signal analysis." He clapped his hands. "We're on a hair-trigger, here, people. This is as real as it gets. Good luck."

Maggie rose with the others. "Maggie Marconi?" a voice said.

She turned. Keller was standing right next to her. "I'm told you used to be great at the NSA," he said. "That is, until you were fired for twice rewriting your superior's conclusions."

Maggie lowered her head. "Sometimes I have a problem with impulse control. But I'm working on it, sir."

"Your conclusions were right, though. Both times. That's why you're getting a second chance." Keller almost smiled. "I've also heard you're the best code breaker there is."

"Thank you, sir," Maggie breathed, flattered. "I won't take it for granted."

"Some people around here think you're a security risk," Keller said. "Don't prove me wrong."

A SAND DUNE, QATAR

Lennox and the other soldiers wearily weighed their options. They had fled to the desert, away from that crazy, killing robot, but they had just half their weapons, a few flares, and a shorted-out portable satellite transmitter. They hadn't heard from anyone else at the demolished SOCCENT base and feared the worst.

One of the soldiers, Epps, stared at the infrared image Fig had snapped of the monster's underbelly. "I've never seen a weapons system like this."

"Yeah, what was that thing?" Fig murmured.

Lennox peered off into the distance. "I don't know, but I doubt it wanted us to survive the attack. If that thing knows we're alive, we're still targets."

"We're the only ones who saw what hit the base," Epps added. "Pentagon's going to want payback."

"It's up to us to get that thermal image back home

ASAP," Lennox concluded. "We have to find some means of communication."

"I think there's a village right over that hill," Fig said. "Maybe . . ."

"It's worth a shot," Lennox agreed. The soldiers started to march across the dunes.

Meanwhile, far away, two Black Hawk helicopters soared over the SOCCENT base. The wreckage was tremendous. Pieces of airplanes lay scattered among squashed Humvees. Twisted, useless communications cables dangled above the destroyed barracks and the dilapidated watchtower. Whoever attacked this base had wiped out its whole crew.

But the Black Hawks didn't search quite close enough. The weakened robot lay beneath a piece of the barracks roof. Sand had blown into the cracks in its armor, and its jaw had frozen in an agonized grimace.

But as night fell, something happened.

Slowly, a mass of steel and wires disengaged from the robot's back and dropped to the ground. The steely jumble began to stretch out and assemble until it formed a giant metal scorpion, with six spindly legs, clawlike drillers, and a lethal stinger tail.

The scorpion thrashed his head back and forth, hungrily scanning the landscape. Then, it noticed the heat signatures of Lennox and the other soldiers, ten miles in the distance.

Someone had survived.

Clicking its metal mandibles together in excitement, the scorpion burrowed into the sand, heading toward them.

Sam pulled up to his friend Miles's house in his banana-yellow Camaro. A toxic black cloud billowed out from the tailpipe.

Sam revved the engine as Miles stepped out onto his porch. "What do you think?" he asked.

Miles wrinkled his nose. "It's . . . yellow."

"Dude, it's old-school!"

He managed to coax Miles into the car. They drove off to the lake, the place where anyone who was anyone from school hung out. As Sam pulled into the parking lot, kids who had been swimming, playing volleyball, or gossiping at the picnic tables stopped, stared at the Camaro, and laughed.

Sam felt uneasy. If *only* someone would bid on his navigational artifacts on eBay—then, he'd have the cash to get this car a decent paint job. Unfortunately, he'd checked his auction before he left. A bunch of people had looked at his stuff, but no one had bid.

As they leaned against the car, Miles nudged Sam in the ribs and pointed. Mikaela Banes waded slowly out of the lake, squeezing water out of her hair. Sam gripped his chest and tried not to swoon.

Then, Mikaela started walking in his direction. As she passed, she made eye contact with Sam. Startled, Sam dropped his keys and managed to mumble "hi." Mikaela didn't answer him, but instead skipped over to Trent DeMarco, who stood behind them next to his giant SUV.

Sam wanted to crawl into a hole and never come out.

Trent grabbed Mikaela and gave her a kiss. Then he noticed Sam staring. Sam quickly looked away, but Trent started to snicker. "Hey, bro!" he called, gesturing to the Camaro. "Sorry about your grandma . . . she died and left you that car, right?"

Sam shrugged. "It's old-school."

Trent squinted at him. "You're the little dude who tried out for the team last semester, right?"

Sam shut his eyes. Trying out for football was the worst mistake he'd ever made. In the very first practice play, four hulking linemen pummeled him, causing his ill-fitting football helmet to pop right off his head. He'd had crushing migraines for days.

"Oh, that?" Sam mustered up. "That was just . . . research. I'm working on a book."

"On what? Sucking at sports?"

"No. On the link between football and brain damage."

Trent lunged for him, but Mikaela grabbed him back. "Stop it."

Trent climbed into his SUV. He patted the passenger seat and looked at Mikaela. "C'mon. There's a frat party. This sucks."

"Lemme drive," Mikaela demanded, pushing her long blonde hair behind her shoulder.

Trent started laughing. "This is a tank! And you're, like, my little bunny. You can't handle this much machine."

Mikaela narrowed her eyes. "I'm your 'little bunny' now?"

"Dude, what's with you?" Trent furrowed his eyebrows.

"Tell you what, *dude*," Mikaela spat. "Get in your daddy-bought car and see if you can find some other little forest creature to patronize! I'll walk home, thanks." She turned around and strode away.

Trent shrugged, started up the car, and peeled out to the street without her.

Sam watched silently as Mikaela stormed by. Suddenly, his Camaro's stereo switched on. A guitar snarled, and the singer crooned, *"Baby, I'm gonna drive you home!"*

Miles and Sam exchanged confused glances. "What's up with your radio?" Miles whispered. But as quickly as the radio came on, it switched off again.

Sam watched as Mikaela took purposeful strides toward the exit, her shoulders down and her jaw set. He grabbed Miles's arm. "Hey," he whispered. "I think my car just sent me a message. *I'm* going to drive her home."

Miles looked at him as if he were nuts. "I'd let her hitchhike. She's so *shallow.*"

Sam slid behind the wheel. "It's ten miles to her house. I'm never gonna get another chance like this again."

"You'd better come back for me," Miles said, kicking one of the Camaro's tires.

Sam pulled the car out of the parking space and slowly, carefully, approached Mikaela, who was nearly at the park's front gate. *Be cool,* he told himself. *Be supercool.*

"Um, hey, Mikaela?" he called, his voice squeaking a little. "Do you need a ride home? 'Cause . . . I was just leaving and . . . you know."

Mikaela looked Sam's car up and down. She seemed disgusted. But finally, she stared up at the darkening sky and then slid into the passenger seat. Sam's heart lifted. *Yesss!*

As Sam pulled out to the main road, Mikaela wrinkled her nose. "Are you wearing cologne?"

Sam blushed. "No. Well . . . yes. It's . . . a little aftershave." He quickly rolled down the window. "You hate it?"

"I'd lighten it up a little," Mikaela answered, giving him an almost smile. "So do we have any classes together?"

"Math . . . gym . . . social studies . . . history," Sam answered.

"Oh," Mikaela said quietly.

The car suddenly stalled. Sam frowned, hit the gas, but it wouldn't budge. When he tried to restart it, the ignition made a coughing sound.

Not now! Sam thought.

"I . . . I know how this looks," he muttered, trying the ignition and then pushing various buttons on the dash, including the air conditioning control and the windshield wipers.

Mikaela gave him a weary look. "Just pop the hood," she said, unhooking her seat belt and getting out.

Sam hit the release latch, and Mikaela lifted up the hood. "Whoa," she said slowly. "This is an aluminum stocker block engine. It's what they use in *race* cars."

"How'd you know that?" Sam asked, looking, too—although to him, understanding car mechanics was about as easy as understanding geometry.

Mikaela shrugged. "My dad. Before he . . . uh . . . left. Serious grease monkey." She gave him a wry smile. "Surprised, huh? I try not to broadcast it. Guys don't like it when you know more about cars than they do."

"Who, like Trent?" Sam asked.

"Maybe."

Sam twisted up his lips. "If Trent drives you crazy, why do you care what he thinks?"

Mikaela turned away. "So maybe I have issues."

She slammed the hood closed. "I think I'll walk home, thanks."

Sam's heart sank to his feet. Things were going so, *so* well, and then he had to ruin it by bringing up Trent. "Um. Okay. See ya," he muttered. Then, he stared up at the heavens. *Please don't let her walk away. Pleeease!*

At that very moment, the Camaro came to life again. The dash lit up, and the motor purred. The radio snapped on, this time playing an oldies station. The singer wailed, *"Darling, don't go!"* and a doo-wop band hummed in the background.

Sam gasped. What was this car's *deal*?

Mikaela whirled around, surprised. She bobbed her head to a few bars of the old song . . . and started to take a few steps back to him.

Sam patted the car's hood. A radio that freakishly turned on by itself was definitely another glitch he'd have to fix. And who knew what else was wrong with this lemon. At this moment, however, he wouldn't trade this car for a million bucks.

AIR FORCE ONE MISSION COMMAND CENTER, 30,000 FEET

Air Force One soared through the night sky. Inside the plane's Secret Service cabin, people worked relentlessly, trying to figure out who had attacked the base in Qatar. No one noticed as the cabin's boom box silently began to reshape.

First, tiny gray feet grew out of its base. Then it began to stretch. The speakers and CD carousel lengthened until it was four-and-a-half-feet tall. It was thinner than a baseball bat, with beady eyes and sharp teeth.

It scuttled into the storage galley and over to an access panel labeled P.O.T.U.S. ONLY. Its spidery fingers picked the lock and tore off the little door to the mainframe terminal. Then, it opened its mouth and let out a shriek. The terminal's monitor blinked to life. CONNECTING TO PENTAGON NETWORK, the screen announced. The creature quickly scanned the files and found the one it wanted: PROJECT ICE MAN: ABOVE TOP SECRET: SECTOR SEVEN ACCESS ONLY. This was the very same file the other robot tried to hack from the Qatar base.

Once the machine finished downloading, it began feeding a new file into the system. TRANSMITTING VIRUS TO PENTAGON NETWORK, the screen said. The creature leaned back and grinned. Soon, everything would be in place.

* * *

Meanwhile, Maggie Marconi sat at a desk at the Pentagon, studying the signal that tried to hack the SOCCENT base system. "You think it's Chinese?" the colleague to her left asked.

Maggie shook her head. "Doesn't sound Chinese. This is . . . something else."

Suddenly, her monitor went crazy. The alert NEW FOREIGN SIGNAL DETECTED flashed across the screen. Maggie sat up straighter. She put her headphones back on and listened to the incoming signal. *This new signal sounded exactly like the one from Qatar!*

She stood up. "They're hacking the network again!"

Her commander raced over. "Run a trace route!"

"I'm trying!" She typed furiously. "It's locking me out!"

A new mess of data erupted on Maggie's screen. Her eyes widened. "Cut the hard lines!" she shrieked, realizing what was happening. "I think they're planting a virus!"

75% . . . 90% VIRUS UPLOAD COMPLETE, the mainframe terminal aboard Air Force One reported. The skinny monster grinned. The operation couldn't have gone more smoothly. Then, suddenly, a force jerked it back. The creature clamped its steely mouth closed. Something had just cut off its connection.

A noise near the elevators made the creature swivel around. Two Secret Service agents burst into the galley. They eyed the mainframe's broken lock and panicked. "Break-in, sector two!" cried one of the agents into her wrist-mic. Then, she spied the spindly monster, crouching behind the prep table. Its beady eyes glowed. She covered her mouth and gasped.

The creature spun behind her and spat out a series of sharp steel discs from its chest. The discs spun through the air like boomerangs, hitting both agents in the legs.

By the time security clamored down the stairs, all was quiet. The wounded agents lay groaning, the strange discs lodged into their legs. Security couldn't figure out where the weapons had come from. Besides the broken lock on the mainframe terminal, everything was status quo. The cabinets were shut, the counters were clean, and the boom box in the corner peacefully played a classical CD.

Whoever had done this must have gotten away.

After the security breach, Air Force One made an emergency landing near D.C. Defense Secretary John Keller, the Chairman of the Joint Chiefs of Staff, the NSA and CIA directors, and other personnel rushed to the scene. They watched out the window as medics carried out the wounded agents.

He turned to the directors. "Okay. So what did they hack?" he asked.

"We still don't know," the NSA director answered.

"And the virus?"

"Well, it isn't affecting our systems, but that could change at any second."

"This is obviously the first phase of a bigger plan," the Chairman of the Joint Chiefs of Staff said. "Presumably a major strike against the United States."

Keller ran his hand through his hair. "Any idea

who we're looking at?"

"Russia and China are the only countries with this kind of capability."

"That's a mistake," Maggie interrupted. The men turned and looked at her, amazed that she'd butt into such an important conversation. Maggie turned to Keller. "Sir, I was just trying to say, it would take twenty years to crack our security codes. No one on *Earth* could do it."

"Yes, but somebody *did* do it." The chairman glowered at her impatiently.

"No, I mean . . ." Maggie wished she could talk to Keller alone. Her hunch was so strange, she feared saying it aloud. "I don't think we should go to war with anyone over this. If I could just have some time to study the signal pattern . . ."

"We have senior intelligence offers on that," Keller snapped. "If you can't muzzle every knee-jerk comment that crosses your mind, I'm taking you out."

He whirled away. Maggie stared at his receding back. "There's more than meets the eye here," she muttered. "I just *know* it."

* * *

Just yards away, beneath Air Force One's wheel well, lurked the alien boom box, once again transformed into its spindly, stretched shape. As a forensics crew boarded the plane to search for evidence of a break-in, the creature raised its head and looked around. It sensed its own kind . . . *somewhere*.

The creature scampered across the tarmac to a police cruiser. The car looked utterly normal, except written in capital letters on the driver's door was the word—or, rather, the name—BARRICADE.

Slowly, the spindly monster slithered into Barricade's front seat, reshaped into a stereo, and eased into an empty slot in the dashboard. A hologram of a mustached man dressed as a police officer flickered to life in the driver's seat. As Barricade rolled to the street, the FBI personnel and Secret Service agents didn't give him a second glance.

The transformed stereo began making a series of bleeps and groans, and the cop car's GPS screen morphed into an eBay auction page. The page's heading said NAVIGATIONAL TOOLS AND HISTORICAL DOCUMENTS!! CIRCA 1897!!! LOOK!! and showed pictures of a pair of spectacles, a sextant, and newspaper clippings about an ice man and an Arctic voyage. Beneath those photos was a picture of the seller himself, a freckled, smallish sixteen-year-old boy. *Sam Witwicky*, said the caption. *Tranquility, U.S.A.*

The stereo made some satisfied clicks, entered Tranquility's coordinates into the GPS, and the car sped away.

WITWICKY HOUSE, TRANQUILITY, U.S.A.

At eleven o'clock that night, Sam's eyes popped open. Did he just hear an engine start? He looked out his window. Someone was in his Camaro!

"Hey, that's my car!" he screamed, leaping out of bed. The thief—a man with a mustache—pulled away.

Sam pulled on a jacket, ran out the door, and steered his bike after him. "Hey!" He pulled his cell phone out of his jacket and dialed the police. "My car's being stolen!" he told the sergeant who answered. "I'm following him right now!"

"Sir, do *not* approach the driver," the sergeant said. "It could be dangerous. We're tracing the call . . . sir?"

But Sam had his phone down at his side. The car had slowed at the gates of the old cement factory. But there was something very, very strange. The man with the mustache had vanished. The car was driving itself!

Sam cowered behind the gate. The Camaro's doors suddenly peeled back, and its trunk sprang open. His car lifted into the air, standing on its back wheels, rising more than twenty feet tall. Sam could just make out the basic shapes of two arms—that *moved*, just like human arms!—two huge legs, and a tiny, barrel-shaped head.

This isn't happening! Sam thought, petrified.

The car reached into its chest, pulled out a flat, shiny disk, and held it in the air. The disk began to glow, and a beam shot out, illuminating the sky with a giant symbol. Sam squinted. It was the same symbol from the Camaro's steering wheel.

Sam heard growling behind him. He turned

just in time to see a Rottweiler snapping at his face, foam dripping from its jaws. Sam jumped back, toppling over a pile of crates, and the dog lunged. Sam pushed himself up and started to run, but the dog was faster. He snatched Sam by the ankle and dragged him backward.

"No!" Sam cried. "Help!"

An engine roared. Sam looked up, and the robot was a Camaro again! The car raced up to Sam and the dog. Confused, the Rottweiler dropped Sam's ankle and started to bark. The Camaro flashed its headlights and gunned its engine. The Rottweiler wriggled, snarled, and bared its teeth, but when the Camaro jerked forward and began to spin doughnuts around Sam, the dog let out a frightened cry and scampered away.

As soon as the Rottweiler disappeared, the Camaro stopped spinning and faced Sam. Its headlights looked like beady eyes, and its grill was a wide, malicious smile. "Please . . . don't kill me," Sam whimpered.

"Freeze!" a voice called. Suddenly, two police officers tackled him. "You're under arrest!"

"Wait!" Sam thrashed as two police officers

tackled him. "Not me! My car, it's . . ."

He desperately pointed to the Camaro, ready to explain the whole bizarre thing. Only . . . the Camaro was gone.

VILLAGE ENCAMPMENT, QATAR

Lennox and the others approached the remote desert village. A high-tension tele-phone pole shuddered. Then an old wood-frame sign creaked and wobbled. It gave way, crashing down nearly on the soldiers' heads. They grabbed their weapons, alert.

The sand beneath Fig's feet started to shake, and the metal scorpion burst through the earth. Fig yelped in surprise, then aimed his rifle at the scorpion and fired into the sand. The scorpion disappeared underground.

"What was that?" Fig whispered.

Before anyone could answer, the monstrous thing erupted out of the ground again, spraying sand everywhere.

"Move, move, move!" Lennox screamed.

The soldiers scattered. The scorpion leaped up again, wildly snapping its mechanical mandibles. Molten flames leaped from its mouth, igniting thatched huts, mud structures, and a shabby clothesline. All the village's goats squealed and scattered.

Lennox grabbed a man who was standing, frozen, watching the horror unfold. "Sir, do you have a phone?" he asked in broken Arabic. "I need to call for help."

"Of course." The man grabbed Lennox's hand. "This way."

He led Lennox to his hut and handed him a cell phone. As soon as a Pentagon operator answered, Lennox screamed, "United States Air Force officer under hostile fire! We're under attack from an unknown aggressor! We need gunships on station and extraction!" He put one finger in his ear to hear better—the noise of the soldiers' and the scorpion's gunfire was deafening.

The operator put him through to an officer. "All right, we're pulling up a real-time image at your GPS coordinates, sir," the officer said.

There was a long pause. Then the officer whispered, "What *is* that?" Lennox could only imagine what the officer saw on his screen: a shadowy, thermal image of his men, helplessly shooting at a giant mechanical scorpion that leaped up and down, under the sand and over their heads. It must have looked insane.

Meanwhile, the scorpion fired pulsing blasts at the soldiers. They advanced and retreated, dodging the flames, trying to fight it off with their remaining artillery. Fig snuck closer to the beast, pummeling it with his laser blaster, when an explosion suddenly launched him into the air. He flew nearly twenty feet, landing on his back, hard. His thermal imager tumbled from his pack, and the scorpion advanced on him.

"Fig!" Lennox cried. The scorpion loomed over Fig's body . . . Fig wasn't moving! Lennox ran closer, his weapon aimed. Suddenly, he heard a roar in the sky. When he looked up, he saw two A-10 fighter planes and an AC-130 gunship soaring right for them. The scorpion looked up, too, and in its momentary distraction, Lennox put his arm around Fig's neck, and then hoisted him onto his back. They rolled safely into a ditch.

The military planes shot missile after missile at the creature. Thick, black smoke and rapid, rhythmic gunfire filled the air. Everywhere smelled like charred computer parts. The smoke got so dense, the soldiers could hardly see a thing, only a thrashing leg here, a flash of the beast's glowing, red eyes there.

Finally, the plane banked and roared away. The men held their breath as the smoke cleared. The beast flailed on the ground, its razor-barbed legs struggling to stand. Two of its antennae were charred beyond recognition, and one of its legs fell off. It burrowed clumsily back under the sand. Lennox let out a relieved sigh.

"That's some freaky wicked machine," Fig cried from behind him, his voice thin and weak.

Lennox turned around and widened his eyes. He hadn't realized how seriously Fig was injured. The scorpion had badly scalded his legs.

Lennox turned to another one of his men. "Get a medevac down here now!" Then, he kneeled down beside Fig. "Stay with me, man," he said. "Please. Stay with me."

9

Sam opened one eye. Sunlight streamed through his window. His clock radio said 2:15 P.M.; he'd slept the whole morning away.

Then he remembered last night. His car had driven itself, transformed into a giant, metal man, beamed something into the sky, stared down an attack dog . . . and then disappeared. Had it been a dream?

The police certainly thought it was. After Sam had explained his story, they thought he was on drugs. They even showed him an antidrug video.

It certainly didn't *feel* like a dream. And he certainly wasn't on drugs.

Sighing, Sam staggered to his computer and logged onto his eBay auction page. Surprise, surprise: zero bids. He stumbled downstairs. When he saw his Camaro, parked obediently in the driveway right in front of the garage door, he backed up into the kitchen table, knocking a bunch of dishes onto the floor.

He grabbed his cell phone. Miles answered on the third ring. "Miles!" Sam screamed. "It's real—it's alive!"

"Whoa, slow down," Miles said. "What's alive?"

"My car! It stole itself, it walked, now it's back, and it's trying to kill me!" Sam glanced apprehensively at the car. It looked normal enough, just sitting there . . . but he knew better. "I'm coming over, Miles. Don't go anywhere."

APARTMENT COMPLEX UNDER P STREET BRIDGE, WASHINGTON, D.C.

Glen Whitman polished off his fourth cheeseburger and restarted his favorite computer game. All he wanted was some downtime. Since his friend and coworker Maggie Marconi vanished a few days ago from Rand, Glen had to take up the brunt of her work.

When the doorbell rang, he groaned in annoyance. To his surprise, Maggie Marconi stood on his porch. Her hair was messy, her clothes were rumpled, and there were huge, dark circles under her eyes.

"Maggie?!" he cried.

Maggie pushed her way inside. "I have to talk to you. No one's better at signal decryption than you are. No one else will believe me."

Glen led her into his bedroom, cleared the burger wrappers off his extra computer chair, and gestured for Maggie to sit down. Maggie pulled a mini CD from her bag. It had a big red CLASSIFIED stamp on the front.

Glen's eyes widened. "Um, are you supposed to have that?"

"It's . . . I borrowed it," Maggie said. "I mean, I'm authorized to know what's on it, I just wasn't supposed to take it from the offices. But I figured the Secret Service will never know."

"Secret Service?" Glen said nervously.

"Help me figure out what this signal is and I'll explain." Maggie slid the CD into the drive. The horrible screech filled the air. Glen pulled up his sound analysis software, and they both watched a sound wave bounce crazily on the screen.

"Signal strength's through the roof," he murmured.

"This signal hacked the Pentagon in less than a minute," Maggie whispered. "That's where I've been the past week: trying to figure out what it is."

"'Less than a minute'?" Glen repeated. "That's impossible.

It'd be like . . . *real* artificial intelligence."

"So where'd this come from?"

"Um . . . science fiction?" Glen suggested.

Maggie looked nervous. "Seriously."

Glen shrugged. "It looks like a machine language . . . but not one I've ever seen before."

Maggie's eyes flickered back and forth. "Just so one of us says this out loud, are we really talking about alien machines here?"

"Who says life on other planets has to evolve from carbon? Why not silicon?" Then Glen pointed at the monitor. "There's something embedded in the signal."

"Gotta be the file they hacked," Maggie said excitedly. "Can you open it?"

Glen furiously typed coding language. In a few seconds, a file name appeared: PROJECT ICE MAN: ABOVE TOP SECRET: SECTOR SEVEN ACCESS ONLY.

"'Project Ice Man'?" Maggie read. "What's Sector Seven?"

Glen opened the file. They stared at a mess of strange, coded symbols they'd never seen before.

"What *is* that?" Glen murmured.

A loud boom filled the foyer. FBI agents burst

through Glen's bedroom door and surrounded them, their guns held high. Glen hid behind the desk.

"Maggie Marconi, you're under arrest for the unauthorized theft of classified information," the first agent said. "You have the right to remain silent . . ."

"Listen!" Maggie protested, as they put handcuffs on both her and Glen. "The enemy signal's a machine language! Maybe even alien! Yes, I know how that sounds, but they downloaded a file, something called 'Sector Seven'—it's some kind of code!"

"Ms. Marconi, you're in enough trouble as it is," the agent warned her.

"Just let me talk to John Keller!" Maggie cried. "Before we go to war with the wrong people!"

But the agents didn't respond. They wordlessly shoved Maggie and Glen into their black car and sped away.

Sam borrowed his mom's bike and pedaled to Miles's house. After a couple blocks, he looked over his shoulder . . . and screamed. His Camaro was following him!

He cut a quick right . . . straight for a tree. "Oof." His front wheel hit the tree hard, and Sam spiraled into the air. He landed hard on his elbow.

"Are you *okay*?"

Mikaela Banes stood over him. Sam saw a flash of yellow out of the corner of his eye. The Camaro was coming! "I gotta go!" he cried, pushing himself up and sprinting away.

Mikaela frowned. Something seemed wrong. She unchained her Vespa scooter from the sign-post and followed him. As she pulled into the street, a police car cut her off.

"Hey!" Mikaela cried at the cop. She knew she shouldn't—yelling at a cop could get her in big trouble. Only this cop didn't even notice her. He had a mustache and stared straight ahead, as if in a trance, and he drove to the end of the street.

Weird, Mikaela thought.

What was even weirder—but what she didn't see—was the eBay Web page on the car's GPS monitor. There was Sam's photo, enlarged to four times its normal size. The words TARGET LOCATED, TARGET LOCATED flashed over Sam's face, again and again.

Sam biked fast across a parking lot jam-packed with cars, constantly looking over his shoulder. He didn't realize that the Camaro was rolling slowly down a parallel aisle, tracking him.

He saw a headlight glare in front of him and realized it was a police car. He was so grateful, he thought he might kiss the policeman. "Officer!" he cried, leaning in to look at the cop, a muscular man with a mustache. "My car's trying to kill me!"

The cop didn't move. Sam frowned. "Hel-*lo*? Are you listening to me?"

He noticed the word BARRICADE emblazoned on the car. Sam wondered what that meant.

"Hello?" Sam cried again. The car angrily jolted forward. Surprised, Sam took his hands off the hood. "Sorry, officer," he stuttered. "I didn't mean any disresp—"

The car made a deafening screech. The doors

moved to the front, the hood moved to the back, the trunk opened to reveal a head, and the seats morphed to become arms. Then the robot stood upright on his back wheels. BARRICADE was now across his chest.

Sam started shaking. Barricade's metal hand swatted him into the air. Sam crashed down on an SUV's windshield, creating a spiderweb crack in the glass. He struggled to slide off the vehicle, but Barricade pinned him down.

"Where are your ancestral artifacts?" Barricade boomed. *"Where are they?"*

Sam's mouth wobbled a few times. "W-wha?"

"Have the Autobots seen the code?"

"I have n-no idea . . . what you're t-talking about . . . ," Sam stuttered.

"You will not live to help them." Barricade lunged, but Sam managed to crawl onto the roof of the SUV and slide to the other side. Sam rounded the corner toward the parking lot's exit and slammed into a girl on a Vespa. Mikaela.

"Mikaela, seriously, run!" Sam screamed. The monster's footsteps behind them sounded like giant hammers ringing against ten-ton blocks of steel.

56

"What's wrong with you?" Mikaela asked. "What's going on?"

Then she looked up. A giant, hulking mass of metal with glowing eyes stood above her. He lifted his foot and stomped her Vespa flat.

Mikaela screamed.

They heard a beep behind them. The Camaro! It gunned its engine, wrenched its wheel, and did a powerslide into Barricade, sending him toppling against a chain-link fence. Then the car wheeled around and faced the kids. Its doors swung open. A silly superhero-style song— *"I am your hero! I've come to rescue you!"*— blared from the speakers.

"Is that your car?" Mikaela cried hysterically. "What's going on?"

The car beeped its horn again. *It wants us to get in,* Sam thought.

The evil robot pushed himself off the fence into a kneeling position. He fixed his eyes on Sam and Mikaela and balled his steel hands into fists.

Sam grabbed Mikaela and pulled her into the Camaro. If he was going to die, he'd rather his Camaro kill him than that crazy robot. The Camaro peeled out. Barricade transformed back into a cop car and started to follow.

They gunned past abandoned, skeletal warehouses and through an old train yard, swerving around burned-out buildings, cinder blocks, and random trash. Barricade rear-ended them, making them skid toward a large pile of bricks. Sam noticed suspicious steel cylinders grow from the cop car's side panels. Blue-green laser beams shot out of them. The Camaro snaked right and left, throwing Mikaela and Sam against the sides of the car like rag dolls.

"Was that a missile?" Sam screamed.

"Think so," Mikaela said. She looked terrified. "This is *not happening!*"

The Camaro drove past a sign that said FUTURE SITE OF TRANQUILITY ESTATES! and into a construction zone. At the end of the road, it spun a 180, lurched to a halt, opened all its doors, and ejected Sam and Mikaela onto the street. They rolled into a chain-link fence, just as the Camaro's sides began to peel back. Metal ground against metal. The car pitched itself on its back wheels, and then grew until it was nearly twenty feet tall, just as it had the night

MEGATRON

OPTIMUS PRIME

BUMBLEBEE

BARRICADE

JAZZ

RATCHET

BLACKOUT

FRENZY

before. Mikaela's eyes widened, and her jaw started to tremble.

Barricade changed back into a robot, too. A flap in his chest opened, and out slithered the long, spindly creature that had infiltrated Air Force One. The monster looked around, noticed Sam and Mikaela, and pounced. Its vinelike fingers snatched their shirt collars and spun them in the air, sending them flying back into the fence.

When Sam opened his eyes, Barricade was storming right for them. "Look out!" Sam cried, shaking Mikaela out of her trance. Barricade raised his fist, ready to strike, but the Camaro robot leaped between him and the kids. Barricade grabbed the Camaro robot and flipped him over his head. The Camaro landed on an aluminum shed, flattening it. He shook himself off, ripped a streetlamp from the ground, and advanced again, swinging the lamp like a baseball bat. He caught Barricade at the knees, sending him sprawling across the road.

Sam was dashing out of the way of the grappling robots, when something pulled him back by the belt loop of his jeans. He turned and saw the spindly monster, jaws snapping. He dragged Sam along the ground and then dropped him at the monster's feet. "Get it off!" Sam cried helplessly.

Mikaela grabbed a power saw from the work site, turned it on, and advanced. "Why don't you come after me, you freak!"

The skinny robot lunged for her. Mikaela swung the saw. Sam scrambled up, found a piece of metal rebar, and—clang!—clobbered the thing on his narrow head. The spindly creature staggered back and then slumped to the ground, making a noise like an engine winding down.

Meanwhile, the Camaro robot's hand transformed into an energy cannon. He fired a burst at Barricade's chest, knocking him backward. Barricade windmilled his arms and took a few more steps back, until he loomed over the edge of a construction pit. The Camaro robot shot one more cannon flare at his enemy, and Barricade toppled over the side with an enormous, earth-shaking crash. Then . . . silence.

The Camaro slowly turned around. He stared at Sam and Mikaela. Sam's heart pounded wildly. Maybe he was as crazy as his great-great-grandfather, but he swore the robot smiled.

Sam took a tentative step in his direction. "What are you doing?" Mikaela hissed.

The robot took a step closer, too. When Sam stopped, he stopped. Sam looked over his shoulder at Mikaela. "I don't think he's gonna hurt us," he whispered.

"Oh, yeah?" Mikaela asked. "You speak robot?"

"I think they want something from me," Sam said. He gestured to Barricade, flat on his back in the construction pit. "That one kept asking me about my 'ancestral artifacts.' And something about a code." He looked at the transformed Camaro. "Can you talk, too?"

The creature shook his head. A voice came through his speakers: "XM Satellite Radio, one hundred thirty digital channels of commercial-free music . . ."

"I think he talks through his stereo," Sam said.

The Camaro nodded his head enthusiastically.

"What were you doing out last night?" Sam asked. "What was that weird symbol you beamed into the sky?"

The creature hesitated. A radio evangelist's

voice came out of the speakers. ". . . and a mighty voice will send a message, summoning forth visitors from heaven!"

"You were calling someone?" Sam prompted.

"And . . . 'visitors from heaven' . . . what're you, like, an alien?" Mikaela asked. The robot squeaked and nodded.

Mikaela and Sam exchanged a bewildered look. An *alien*?

Then, the robot morphed back into the Camaro. All of his doors opened. Sam looked at Mikaela. "I think it wants us to get in."

Mikaela nervously stepped back. "And go where?"

"I don't know, but think about it," Sam said. "Fifty years from now, when we're looking back at our lives, don't you wanna be able to say we had the guts to do it?"

Mikaela took a long, hard look at the car. "Okay . . . "

As they drove away from the construction site, Mikaela touched the symbol on the steering wheel. "Wait," she said to the car. "If you can, like, reshape yourself, why did you pick such an ugly yellow thing? I mean, you can be anything, right?"

The Camaro slammed his brakes and ejected Sam and Mikaela onto the sidewalk. Sam glowered at her. "Great. I think you hurt his feelings."

The Camaro scanned the street, jumping from car to car, analyzing. Finally, he focused on a brand-new Camaro GTO, measured the car's exact dimensions, and within seconds, began to reshape. He became less boatlike and more muscular and sleek. The rust on his body vanished. He drove over to the kids and beeped the brand-new horn.

Mikaela jumped in. "Now *this* is a car!"

A burning comet spiraled from deep space, hurtling past stars and moons. When it hit Earth's atmosphere, it cracked into four separate, fire-hot orbs, scattering in different directions.

One of the orbs landed behind the baseball stadium, another near a streetside café, and still another on a family's front lawn. The fourth and final fiery ball landed near Sam, Mikaela, and the brand-new Camaro, just as they pulled away from the construction site. Instinctively, Mikaela fearfully grabbed Sam. Then she realized what she was doing and recoiled.

"Sorry," Mikaela said quickly.

"It's cool," Sam answered, hoping he didn't sound too eager.

The fiery ball skidded a few football fields before finally rolling to a stop close to them. The Camaro slowly approached it. What looked like a meteorite from far away was actually a pulsating silver sphere. Liquid hot silver beads oozed off its side, forming a noxious, burbling puddle. Slowly, the puddle began to rise up and organize itself, forming a shape.

A metallic leg and foot arose first. Then an arm, then the top of a head. The thing lengthened, rising above the trees. Only it didn't look like the Barricade or the Camaro robots. It was a raw mass of intersecting wires, LEDs, and circuit boards.

This day just gets weirder and weirder, Sam thought.

The massive silver exoskeleton glanced at an eighteen-wheeler on the highway. It narrowed its eyes, did a quick scan, and transformed into the truck's carbon copy, just as the Camaro had transformed moments ago.

Mikaela nudged Sam. "Call me crazy, but something tells me that thing and your car are from the same planet."

Miles away, another skeletal robot staggered through a back alley behind the baseball stadium until it came to an exotic car lot. The robot scanned a sports car rotating behind thick bulletproof glass. Transforming took fewer than five seconds.

Behind the outdoor café, the third exoskeleton perked up as a Search and Rescue vehicle passed. In a puff of smoke, the robot became an ambulance, too.

The fourth robot stood up in the suburban house's front yard and brushed mowed grass off its body. A powerful pickup truck in the driveway caught its eye. Instantly, a duplicate truck roared off the grass and onto the street.

The eighteen-wheeler drove over to Sam and Mikaela. It transformed again, this time into a mighty towering robot, much taller than the other robots they had seen so far. Sam and Mikaela got out of the Camaro and took a nervous step back, not sure if this robot was good or evil, but the robot paid them no attention. He turned toward the highway, hands on hips, as if waiting for something.

Three cars appeared. The ambulance led the way, then the sports car, and then the pickup. The vehicles drove right up to the robot and stopped. The Camaro left Sam and Mikaela and rolled into line beside the others.

Whoa, Sam thought. *Whatever message my car*

sent out last night, it sure got a response.

The large, silvery robot turned to Sam. "Samuel James Witwicky?" he boomed in a deep, powerful voice. "Descendant of Archibald Amundsen Witwicky, captain of the sailing vessel *Discovery*?"

"Y-yeah . . . ," Sam squeaked.

"I am Optimus Prime."

"You—you speak English?" Mikaela stammered.

"We have assimilated Earth's languages through your World Wide Web."

"Wow, you are aliens," Sam whispered.

"Correct," Optimus answered. "We are autonomous robotic organisms from the planet Cybertron."

"Autonomous robots," Mikaela repeated. *"Autobots."*

"Do you, um, all have names?" Sam looked at the other vehicles.

"Yes." Optimus turned to the sports car. "My first lieutenant. Designation: Jazz."

"Greetings," Jazz said, revving his souped-up engine.

Optimus pointed at the pickup truck. "Our weapons specialist, Ironhide."

"This exoskeleton seems suitable for battle," Ironhide said.

"And our medical officer, Ratchet," Optimus said, gesturing to the Search and Rescue vehicle. "And you already know Bumblebee, your guardian."

"'Bumblebee'?" Sam stared at the Camaro.

The famous Muhammad Ali catchphrase rang out from the Camaro's speakers. "'Float like a butterfly, sting like a bee.'"

Mikaela frowned. "If you can talk, why can't Bumblebee?"

"His vocal processor was destroyed on the battlefields of Tyger Pax," Ratchet explained.

"Oh, right," Sam said, as if that made perfect sense.

"We come in search of the Allspark, a supreme power that imbues us with the gift of 'Spark,'" Optimus said.

"It's the life force within all Transformers," Ratchet added.

"We must find the Allspark before Megatron does," Optimus said.

"Who's Megatron?" Sam asked.

Optimus paused, looking up into the sky. "Once, we were brothers, united. Twin sons among the dynasty of Primes. But greed twisted him into a servant of evil. He turned his armies against us. For their betrayal, they bear the name *Decepticons.*"

"Yikes," Mikaela whispered.

"They may already be here," Optimus said. "You may have already seen them."

Sam told them about the cop car Bumblebee vanquished in the construction pit, and the scrawny, spindly thing that they knocked senseless.

"That sounds like Barricade and Frenzy," Jazz said.

Barricade! Sam thought. That was printed on the mechanoid's chest! "So . . . what's so bad about Megatron?" he asked.

"Megatron feeds on the Sparks of vanquished ones, growing stronger with each one he consumes," Optimus explained. "The war nearly extinguished our race. Those who survived were forced to flee. Megatron was the first to follow the Allspark's signal here before succumbing to the ice . . . where your ancestor encountered him."

Sam suddenly got it. "Wait! That's what great-great-grandpa saw on his voyage! He thought Megatron was the Ice Man!"

"Exactly," Optimus said. "Your great-great-grandfather accidentally triggered Megatron's navigational system, which holds the coordinates to the Allspark's location on Earth."

"The beam blinded him," Jazz said, "but it left a coded imprint of the map as well."

"What do you mean 'coded imprint'?" Sam asked.

"On his glasses," Optimus explained.

Sam blinked. "On his glasses?" he repeated. "The map to this Allspark thing is *on his glasses*?" He shook his head in disbelief. "So how did you know where to find me? Or that I had his glasses?"

"eBay," Ironhide answered.

Sam widened his eyes. "No way."

Optimus earnestly clasped his enormous hands together. "If we are first to reach the Allspark, we will return it to our home world and use it to rebuild our race. If Megatron finds it, he'll use it to transform your planet's machinery into a new legion of Decepticons. Their mission will be to conquer the universe . . . starting with Earth."

Mikaela gasped and looked at Sam. "Please, please, *please* tell me you have those glasses."

"I do," Sam whispered. He just hoped he could get them in time.

ennox and his soldiers watched as white fluffy clouds passed them by. They were heading back to the United States. Three research and development scientists stood in the middle of the plane's cabin, staring at a piece of the giant mechanical scorpion's tail they'd hefted onto a stainless steel research table. Although badly damaged, the scorpion's tail had begun to regenerate; slowly but surely it was growing longer and longer.

"Unbelievable," said one of the scientists. "It's like some kind of self-regenerating molecular armor."

"But look here, where the high-heat laser melted right through him," Lennox whispered, pointing to a part of the creature's leg. As he leaned closer to look, the tail suddenly moved. The deadly spike on the end lashed back and forth wildly, nearly clipping Lennox's nose. Everyone jumped back, throwing their bodies against the wall. But the scorpion was still again.

"Just a reflex," one of the scientists murmured, ". . . I hope."

Lennox looked at Epps. "Get on the radio with northern command—our most effective weapon was high-heat laser rounds. I recommend we load 'em in all our gunships."

A medical sergeant appeared from behind the mobile-infirmary curtain and grabbed Lennox's arm. He gestured toward the other side of the curtain and sadly shook his head. Lennox's heart dropped. It was Fig.

Lennox pushed back the curtain. Fig lay on a stretcher, pale and almost gray. He was near death, everyone knew. There was nothing anyone could do for him. "Hey, amigo," Lennox called softly.

Fig winced out a smile. "Not gonna get that perfect day, am I, Sarge?"

Lennox took Fig's hand and tried to be strong. "You kidding? We're almost there, man. Just breathe easy. This time next week, you'll be kicking your board over turquoise waters."

Fig's breathing slowed. His face began to relax.

"Light, offshore breeze," Lennox said. "And here

comes the wave ... sweeps you up, you ride the tube all the way down the coast ... right into the sunset." He paused. "There it is, your perfect day."

Fig smiled ... then slipped away. Lennox rose up and stared angrily out the window. Whoever had built those killing machines back there in the desert was going to pay.

WITWICKY HOME, TRANQUILITY, U.S.A.

Sam, Mikaela, and Bumblebee quietly rolled up to the Witwicky house. The other Autobots—Optimus, Jazz, Ratchet and Ironside—followed.

"Keep them quiet while I get the glasses," Sam whispered to Mikaela, his hand on the knob of the front door. "I'll be right back."

He crept upstairs to his room and began rummaging for the glasses case. Suddenly, his whole room was in shadow. Optimus stood at the window, lifting Mikaela from the ground to Sam's windowsill. "You must help him look," Optimus said to her, as she climbed in.

Sam froze in terror. Not because there were alien robots outside his window, or because the world might end if he didn't find the glasses . . . but because Mikaela, the girl he had a crush on, was the first girl ever to step inside his room. He snatched up a pair of boxers and quickly threw them in the closet.

"So, um, yeah. This is my room," Sam said, leaning casually against his bureau, shoving another pair of boxers in the drawer.

"It's nice," Mikaela answered politely.

Sam continued to rummage. His face darkened. "It's not here."

"What do you mean?" Mikaela whispered.

"My glasses were in my backpack, I'm sure of it. But it isn't here."

"Have you found them?" Optimus's voice boomed. The other Autobots crowded behind him at the window.

"Shhh!" Sam hissed. He bit his lip. "No, I don't know where my backpack is!"

"Continue searching!" Optimus ordered.

"You have to get out of here!" Sam shooed them away. "And don't stomp on my mom's flowers!"

Optimus turned to the others. "Autobots. Fall back."

The Autobots retreated into the yard. Sam tore around his room some more. When he looked out the window, however, he noticed that Optimus had transformed back into truck form . . . on his front lawn!

He knocked on the window. "That's not hiding!" What was Optimus thinking? Semis didn't park on lawns! That was as bad as parking in the kitchen!

Suddenly, it hit Sam: *the kitchen*. He'd left his backpack on the kitchen table! He grabbed Mikaela's hand, ran down into the kitchen, found his backpack, and unzipped the front pocket. He held up the glasses case for Mikaela to see. She gave him a relieved grin.

Then, the doorbell rang.

Sam and Mikaela looked at each other. It couldn't be Optimus, could it?

The doorbell rang again. Sam sprinted to the door. If he got there first, he could just tell Optimus to leave. Hopefully the neighbors hadn't seen him. Then, out of the corner of his eye, he saw his dad coming down the stairs. He was much closer to the door than Sam was. Sam catapulted over the living room couch, knocking over a vase of flowers, but now his dad's hand was on the doorknob.

Thankfully, it was just a group of men in stuffy suits standing at the other side.

"Ronald Wickity?" one of the men asked. "Sam Wickity?"

"It's Witwicky," Sam's father said apprehensively. "Who are you?"

He flashed a badge with a strange insignia. "Name's Simmons. We're with the government. Sector Seven." He looked over his shoulder at Sam.

"It's *Witwicky*," Sam reminded him. He peeked around the men. Thankfully, Optimus was no longer on the front lawn.

"What's going on?" Mr. Witwicky asked, stepping out to the porch.

Sam followed him. Another agent swiped a Geiger counter along the flowers beneath Sam's window—where Optimus and the others had stood. "I'm getting massive readings," the agent called.

"Get a sample," Simmons snapped. Then he turned to Mr. Witwicky and gave him a gruff, suspicious look. "Your son filed a stolen car report last night. We have reason to believe it involves a national security matter."

"What?" Mr. Witwicky cried. "Why?"

Sam widened his eyes in terror. *National security matter?*

"We can't explain why, sir." One agent grabbed Sam by the shoulder; another grabbed Mikaela. "But both of these kids are going to have to come with us."

Keller stood in the middle of the throng of agents and technicians. This room in the Pentagon had been set up as central command: Huge overhead screens showed satellite feeds of worldwide naval activity, and the words *attack* and *war* fluttered through the air. He'd just received a brief that Chinese and United States task forces were approaching one hundred nautical miles of cruise missile range. A knot formed in his stomach. He didn't want to go to war with anyone, but if this was what they had to do . . .

The Chairman of the Joint Chiefs of Staff tapped Keller. "Sir, this is Agent Tom Banachek, from the White House." He gestured to a scowling man with a titanium briefcase strapped to his wrist. "He's with Sector Seven."

"I've never heard of it," Keller barked, annoyed. He didn't have time to chitchat with random White House people.

"I'm here under direct order from the president, sir," Banachek said smoothly. "He's instructed us to brief you himself."

"Now?" Keller felt weary. "On what?"

FAILURE, FAILURE, FAILURE, all of the monitors suddenly screamed. That message meant the system firewalls had locked up to protect the system's integrity. Keller grabbed a general. "What's happening?"

The general looked worried. "Communications are out. I think the virus just activated!"

Keller's stomach dropped. "How much is it disrupting?"

"Well . . . everything," the general said. "Satellite and landlines are all down. Total network failure."

"What do you mean 'everything'?" Keller asked. "Phones, TV, Internet, all communication forms everywhere?" But from the look on the general's face, he knew that was *exactly* what he meant.

"Sir." Banachek gestured to his briefcase. "I think you need to see what I have in here. Now."

Banachek typed in a four-digit code to unlock the briefcase on his wrist. He snapped a laptop terminal open, unfolded a tiny antenna, and turned to Keller.

"Sector Seven was convened in secret under President Hoover more than eighty years ago, for one reason and one reason alone," Banachek said. *"Aliens are real."*

Keller flinched. *What did he say?*

Banachek smirked. "You might remember that, in 2003, NASA lost contact with the Mars rover? We told them to report the mission a failure? Well, there were a few images that rover was able to retrieve, after all."

He brought up a pixilated video feed that showed the Mars rover's leg in the foreground and the planet's barren, rocky terrain in the background. Then the camera panned over a few feet . . . to a giant, mechanical man, leg raised, ready to stomp the lens to bits. Then, abruptly, the picture went to static.

Keller gasped.

"We think this is the one that hit Qatar," said Banachek.

Keller couldn't breathe. Something was coming. And they were running out of time.

DOWNTOWN TRANQUILITY, U.S.A.

Sam thought the Sector Seven Suburban was sweet: a rear-seat DVD player, climate-controlled air conditioning, cushy leather seats. Any other time, he would've been psyched to be in such a pimped-out ride. Not today.

Sam tried to stay calm: *He* hadn't done anything wrong. It wasn't like it was *his* fault the Autobots found him. He had just put some stuff up on eBay!

And yet, if they weren't in trouble, why were they here?

He tried to calm himself down by watching the news broadcast on TV. The reporter talked about strange meteorite sightings at a baseball game, on a busy city street, and in a suburban neighborhood. Abruptly, the feed went dead.

"Simmons here," Simmons barked into his cell phone. "I need a code black . . . we've got the boy." Suddenly, he held the phone from his ear. "Hello?"

he shouted at it. "Hel-*lo*?" He threw the phone against the dashboard in frustration.

Then Simmons whirled around and smiled sinisterly at Sam. "So, last night at the police station, you told the officer your car . . . transformed. Enlighten me."

"T-this is a big misunderstanding," Sam stuttered. "When I said it transformed, I meant it went from being my car to being my *stolen* car . . ."

"What do you kids know about aliens?" Simmons interrupted.

"Aliens?" Sam's voice squeaked. "Don't believe in 'em."

"Total crap," Mikaela added quickly.

Simmons eyed Sam. "Your great-great-grandfather believed in them, though, didn't he?"

"Oh, well, you know," Sam answered, his mouth dry. "He was nuts."

Simmons stared at them. His nostrils flared in and out. "Why do I think you know something?" He glared at Mikaela. "And I don't think you'd want to test me. Especially not with your juvenile record."

Sam turned to Mikaela. "What's he talking about?"

Mikaela looked horrified. "Nothing."

Simmons made a *tsk* sound with his tongue. "Grand theft auto? That ain't nothing!"

"What?" Sam squeaked, looking at her.

Mikaela put her hands over her face and sighed. "Okay, so those cars my dad taught me to fix? They weren't always his."

"Your dad taught you to steal cars?" Sam gasped.

"No," Mikaela said sharply. "I didn't steal them. I just didn't testify against him, so they made me an accessory."

"Wow," Sam snickered. "You must be totally screwed up."

Rage rushed into her face. "Thanks a lot! How'd you like it if I said you must be a total geek runt for not making the football team!"

"Hey!" Sam cried, embarrassed.

"Pay attention." Simmons clapped his hands and pointed at Mikaela. "A record like yours could land you in jail or get you kicked out of school. Colleges will never touch you. Pucker up and kiss your life good-bye, missy."

Mikaela bit back tears. "Leave her alone!" Sam

shouted. "Look, I'll tell you what's going on, but you're not gonna believe it."

Simmons stared at him, the corners of his thin lips curling into a smile. "Give it a whirl, kiddo. I'm all ears."

Thonnkkk! A giant foot slammed down right in front of them, blocking the road. The SUV skidded to a halt. "What the . . . ?" Simmons cried.

The SUV's roof started to tremble . . . and something lifted the whole car off the ground! Sam and Mikaela looked out the window. There was Optimus, holding the puny roof between his fingers. The other Autobots, now transformed into robots, stood menacingly behind him.

"Oooh, you're in tuh-*rub*-ble now," Sam singsonged softly.

Optimus set the SUV back on the ground and popped off the roof, as easily as opening the top of a can of soda. "Out of the vehicle," he commanded.

All the agents spilled from the car, except for Simmons, who didn't seem particularly surprised that Optimus existed. "I'm not authorized to communicate with you," he said stubbornly.

Jazz grabbed a pair of handcuffs from the Suburban's front seat. He dropped them in front of Mikaela. "Lock him up."

"Gladly." Mikaela grinned, pulled Simmons out of the car, and cuffed one hand to a streetlight. She pulled the cuffs tight enough for Simmons to wince. "*That's* for calling me a thief."

Simmons glared at Mikaela, Sam, and the Autobots. "You're going to regret this in a big way."

Mikaela giggled. "Man, if only Trent could see me now."

Sam's mouth fell open. "Wait. Did you just say *Trent*?"

Mikaela shrugged and avoided eye contact. "Yeah. So?"

"We—we discovered an alien race together, and you still care what he thinks about you?" Sam cried.

Mikaela scowled. "What are you, my therapist?"

Sam couldn't believe he'd been so stupid. "We're going to possibly save the world, but we'll go back to school Monday morning and nothing's gonna change, is it? I'll still be the invisible guy with gummy worms in my hair . . . and you'll go back to being shallow."

"*I'm* shallow?" Mikaela lunged for him. "I gave up my whole future because I wouldn't turn in my dad. When have you ever had to sacrifice anything in your perfect little life?"

Sam took a step back. She was right. But before he could apologize, two choppers crested the hillside. More Suburbans screeched in, surrounding them.

"See?" Simmons sneered, as one of the new agents dashed out of the Suburban and cut him free. "Now *you're* in tuh-*rub*-ble."

The chopper's headlights raked Optimus's form. Optimus reached down, plucked Mikaela and Sam from the ground, and hiked them up to his shoulder.

"Hold on," he commanded. He and the other Autobots pulse-blasted the Suburban's tires and sprinted away.

They ran through Tranquility's streets. Sam and Mikaela, grasping at Optimus's armor for dear life, flapped painfully up and down with each of Optimus's footfalls. As one of the choppers gained on them, Optimus raised his wrist, and shot out a gray billowing smokescreen cloud. By the time the chopper found its way through the cloud, the Autobots had safely hid on the cliffs under a bridge.

The chopper searched and searched, circling dangerously close to the Autobots without seeing them. Mikaela and Sam scrambled and scratched to keep a good hold of Optimus. Sam watched as his glasses case slid out of his pocket and fell down, down, down . . . until it plopped onto the highway far below.

Mikaela's hands gave out. As she slid down Optimus's body, Sam grabbed her wrist and tried to pull her back up. Mikaela dangled, feet swinging. "Don't let me go!" she screamed to Sam.

"I can't hold on!" Sam gritted his teeth. His fingers began to cramp and slowly straighten.

Bumblebee saw all this from his hiding spot at the top of the bridge. Just as Sam's last finger broke free and the kids began to fall, he spun around, transformed into a robot, and made a swan dive for the ground. He stuck out his palm like a baseball glove, and Sam and Mikaela landed inside.

"Thanks," Sam whispered, after Bumblebee

gently set them on the ground.

Then they heard a cry from the chopper overhead. "Do it now!"

Steel mesh nets dropped down. One looped tightly around Bumblebee's arm; the other snagged his legs. Bumblebee's mouth twisted into a confused frown. Moving made the nets cinch even tighter. The Autobot's knees buckled, and his torso wriggled. The chopper began to move, dragging Bumblebee along the pavement.

Sam stared at the chopper. "What are you doing? You're hurting him!" He rushed to Bumblebee and clawed at the nets.

"Get back!" a Sector Seven agent cried, grabbing Sam.

Two agents zip-lined down from the chopper. They held large, thick hoses connected to backpack canisters full of liquid nitrogen. They surrounded Bumblebee, hit a switch on the canisters, and began to spray. As soon as the liquid hit Bumblebee, the robot arched his back in agony.

"He's not hurting anyone!" Sam screamed, thrashing around in the agent's arms.

Optimus crept up to meet the other Autobots

at the top of the bridge. All eyes were on Bumblebee and the chopper. "We have to help him!" Jazz urged.

Optimus closed his chrome eyes. "We cannot engage without harming the humans!"

"But . . ."

"Stand down," Optimus roared. "We do not harm humans. That's an order."

The chopper began to rise, pulling the nets—and Bumblebee—with it. The chopper struggled against Bumblebee's weight, bouncing around at strange angles, until it found its stability and lifted up above the clouds. Bumblebee was now motionless, his nitrogen-soaked body glistening.

The Autobots watched helplessly as Bumblebee zoomed out of sight. The Sector Seven agents shoved Sam and Mikaela into another Suburban and raced away. Optimus lowered his eyes, feeling heavy-hearted. Then, he noticed a glasses case, lying abandoned on the ground. He crept out from under the bridge, plucked it from the pavement, and opened it up.

The glasses were nestled inside. Optimus could see the code etched on their lenses.

TRANQUILITY ESTATES CONSTRUCTION SITE, TRANQUILITY, U.S.A.

Night fell. Amid the construction site wreckage, Barricade lay motionless in the pit where Bumblebee had defeated him. Slowly, the very tip of his finger moved. His hand formed a fist.

A few feet away, the spindly robot called Frenzy lay splayed out on the pavement. The Decepticon opened his eyes and leaped up, just as Barricade was struggling out of the construction pit.

"The virus has executed its programs," Barricade said in their shared, strange alien language. "Global communications are off-line."

Frenzy smiled. "It's time to summon the others."

He opened his mouth and emitted a screechy wail, too high-pitched for human ears to hear. The sound spread far and wide over the Earth. At an army base, an F-22 Raptor fighter jet heard the sound and started to move. His name: Starscream. In a tank graveyard, an M-1 Abrams tank thought to be out of commission slowly awoke. This was Brawl. And at another military base, among rows of artillery, tanks, and trucks, a mine-clearing vehicle named Bonecrusher heard the call and revved to life. Steel mandibles protruded from his front, and he crashed through the fence.

All three vehicles raced toward the signal, ready for battle.

O ptimus studied the code imprinted on Captain Witwicky's glasses. "The Allspark is two hundred fifty miles from our position," he said, feeling hopeful because they were so close. The others looked at him forlornly.

"I can't believe we let them take Bumblebee," Jazz said.

"We're not like the Decepticons," Optimus replied. "We never harm humans."

"And if the humans harm *him*?"

"Bumblebee knows the risks of our war," Optimus said. "He would want us to complete our mission."

Ratchet moved closer. "If we face Megatron, can you bring yourself to destroy your own brother?"

Optimus sighed. It had been ages since he had faced Megatron—but now it was time. "I will do what I must."

BLACK HAWK CHOPPER CABIN, 20,000 FEET

The agents had had Maggie and Glen in an interrogation room in the Pentagon for more than six hours until, suddenly, several guards burst through the door, uncuffed them, and wordlessly whisked them to a Black Hawk chopper. Maggie kept asking where they were going, but no one would answer. When she climbed aboard and saw Keller, her jaw dropped.

"You were right, Maggie," Keller said solemnly. "You were right all along."

Agent Banachek from Sector Seven filled her in on what was happening. With every word, Maggie grew paler. *Aliens. Hacking our systems. Cutting off communication. Attacking the Earth.* Her hairbrained theory was actually *right.*

Banachek didn't explain where they were going. Maggie stared nervously out the window until something familiar and monumental caught her eye. A huge waterfall. Massive generators. They were landing at the top of the Hoover Dam.

Two more choppers arrived, and Maggie studied the people getting out of them: a teenage boy and girl and a grumpy-looking man in a suit from one, a well-built soldier in camo fatigues from the other. Keller exited the chopper and strode across the tarmac to shake the soldier's hand. "We got your intel, Captain Lennox," he said. "Excellent work!"

"Thank you, sir!" Lennox answered. He, too, had been briefed as to what was going on: The creature that attacked the Qatar base was an alien fighter, and others like it had shut down communications—meaning he hadn't been able to get in touch with his wife to tell her he was alive. All he wanted to do was go home, but the aliens wanted more, and Lennox promised to help fight them however he could.

"Did you get my message about the gunships?" Lennox asked.

"Being retrofitted with high-heat lasers right now," Keller said. His face clouded over. "Although, it won't do much good if we can't get communications back up."

A few feet away, Sam wriggled out of Simmons's arms. "Get your hands off me!"

Banachek walked up to them and put his hand on Sam's shoulder. "Son," he started.

"Just take me to my car!" Sam shouted. "Give me back Bumblebee!"

"Listen," Banachek said. "People could die. We need to know everything you know."

Sam shook his head. "Not until you promise me you won't hurt Bumblebee."

Banachek paused; the other agents had told him the boy had a strange affection toward the alien they'd captured. "All right. We'll do only passive scan tests on him, okay?"

"Another thing." Sam pointed at Mikaela. "You have to erase her record. Forever."

Mikaela gasped in surprise, and Sam gave her a brief smile. Even if Mikaela went back to Trent on Monday, even if she never spoke to him again and hurled gummy bears at his head, at least he'd know he'd done the right thing.

"Fine," Banachek said after a moment. "Now. Everyone come with me."

Banachek led them to a group of elevators, took them down six flights, and strode into a generator room. "Here's the situation," he said in a low voice. "We're facing war against a technological civilization far superior to our own. You've all had direct contact with these things, which makes you the world's experts on how to beat them."

"They have a name," Sam piped up. "They're called Transformers."

Banachek looked at him carefully. "They told you that?"

Sam nodded. "Yeah. Some of them are good guys. We're tight."

Banachek led everyone down a long, sloped, spooky tunnel. "With communications down, you're our last line of defense. No more secrets. Starting now."

They came to a door. Banachek felt around for a keypad, typed in a code, and the door slid open. Everyone blinked in the bright light. They were in a huge, echoing silo. A giant robot stood in the middle of the room, hooked up to serious gauges, monitors, and liquid nitrogen tubes.

Maggie screamed.

"I'll be . . . ," Keller murmured.

Sheets of ice paralyzed the robot's body. His arms had frozen in mid-swipe, his legs in mid-stomp, and his face in a silent scream. A huge, masklike emblem splashed across his chest. Sam recognized him right away.

"We call him 'N.B.E. One,' or Nonbiological Extraterrestrial One," Banachek whispered. "He was the first we found."

"That's not his real name," Sam said triumphantly. "This is Megatron. He's the leader of the Decepticons."

"The head of the bad guys," Mikaela added.

"He's been in cryo-stasis for nearly a hundred years," Banachek said.

"A hundred years?" Keller turned to Banachek. "You didn't think I might need to know you were keeping a hostile alien robot frozen in the basement of . . . of the Hoover Dam?"

"President's discretion, sir," Banachek said apologetically. "Roosevelt never told Truman he had the atomic bomb. And until now, N.B.E. One had never been a credible threat to national security."

"So . . . why did he come to Earth?" Lennox asked.

Sam raised his hand. He knew this one. The others looked at him impatiently, and he instantly put his hand down, embarrassed. "Um, he's looking for something called the Allspark. They all are."

"Did you say 'Allspark'?" Banachek said.

"Uh-huh," Sam said.

Banachek's face clouded over. He glanced over at Simmons, who shifted his eyes to the right and clamped his mouth shut.

Sam's mouth fell open. "You guys know where it is?!"

"Better than that," Simmons said. "We have it here."

* * *

They walked through another series of tunnels and came to an observation deck. The Allspark, encased in a thick sheet of glass, pulsated and buzzed. Strange, alien glyphs covered all its six sides. Hoses and wires attached the Allspark to a series of monitors, gauges, and pumps. Bio-suited technicians sat at each monitor, never taking their eyes off the readouts.

"Whoa," Sam whispered. This thing was awesome.

"We didn't find it until 1920," Banachek whispered. "President Hoover had the dam built around it—a perfect way to keep the Allspark's energy from being detected."

"What do you mean by 'energy'?" Maggie asked.

Banachek pointed to the MP3 player on Glen's belt. "You see that? Innocent little gadget, right? This Allspark can harness the power of machines—any machine. Its energy could turn that thing into a killer that could wipe out all of you."

Glen laughed, a little apprehensively.

Mikaela turned to Sam, her eyes wide. "Don't you remember what Optimus said? Megatron was going to use the Allspark's energy to harness our world's machinery to take over the Earth!"

Sam held his breath and then, fearfully, thought of Optimus. *If only they were here,* he thought, *this could all be over, right now.*

Maggie walked the whole way around the Allspark, examining each side. Its glyphs looked so familiar. "These markings . . . do you know what they are?"

"Some kind of symbolic language," Banachek said. "Identical to the transmission we pulled off Megatron's data log and put into our secret government files."

"Yeah, that was a map to the Allspark," Sam explained.

"These same markings and patterns were hacked off Air Force One," Maggie said.

Mikaela and Sam looked at each other apprehensively. Optimus and the Autobots hadn't hacked anything off Air Force One. It had to have been the Decepticons. "They know it's here," Mikaela whispered, the blood draining from her cheeks.

Suddenly, the control room stared to shake, knocking Sam, Mikaela, and the others off balance. Lights popped and exploded like tiny supernovas, and everything went dark.

"Looks like they've arrived," Keller said.

Frenzy's eerie signal led the Decepticon warriors straight to the Hoover Dam. Starscream, the fighter jet, cruised over the dam's gushing waterfalls and dropped a barrage of missiles on the largest generators. The dam compound shook, causing everyone inside to panic.

"Nellis Air Force Base is fifty miles away!" Keller shouted, shielding his head from the falling ceiling panels. "We can have air support in ten minutes."

Blackout, the Decepticon chopper that had decimated the Qatar base, had flown all the way from the Middle East to join Starscream in the air assault. He sent a guided missile into the water basin, creating an instant tidal wave. Another rumble went through the ceiling and the floor.

Sam stepped between everyone. "Is my car here?"

Banachek hesitated. "Well, yes, but we're studying it."

"Bumblebee's not an 'it,'" Mikaela said. "He's a *him*."

"You have to take me to him!" Sam cried. "He can get the Allspark out of here safely!"

Simmons laughed. "What are you, nuts? We don't know what'll happen if we let it near the Allspark! It could go berserk!"

"Didn't you hear us?" Sam balled up his fists. "If we don't get the Allspark outta here, our planet is toast!"

Lennox put up his hands. "It's worth a shot. If he's wrong, we're dead anyway."

"No!" Simmons snarled. "These kids are delinquents! Why should we believe . . ."

"That's *enough*," Lennox said roughly. "I've got a baby I've never even seen. I want to go home. *Now take the kid to his car!*"

"Fine." Simmons nodded to Banachek, who led them through a series of tunnels. Finally, they got to another door and entered another giant silo. In the corner, inside a gigantic jar, lay Bumblebee, as a robot, looking defeated and scared.

Banachek walked over to one of the scientists, and whispered something, and the scientist walked to Bumblebee's overhead hatch. "Stand clear!" he cried, pressing the release.

Bumblebee looked up fearfully as the hatch of the jar opened. Then his binds unlocked with a clank. Sam ran to Bumblebee and wrapped his arms around Bumblebee's leg. "The Allspark's here!" Sam whispered. "And the Decepticons are coming!"

Bumblebee stood up, alert. He took a tentative step into the center of the room. The scientists all stood there, arms uneasily crossed over their chests. Bumblebee stretched out his back, and then started to run.

They heard another deafening boom. Debris crumbled from the walls. More things shook and burst. "How are we going to call for backup if all our communications systems are down?" Keller yelled to Banachek, as everyone ran for the exit.

"Wait!" Maggie cried, getting an idea as they passed a computer room. "Glen! Can you hot-wire computer equipment to transmit Morse code?"

"I—I dunno," Glen said, seeming flustered. "Why?"

Maggie pulled him into the computer room and pointed to a cluster of machines. "The military guard frequency—it's a shortwave channel. We could use it to call air support!"

"Great!" Lennox cried. "You get our birds in the air, and when we get wherever we're going, we'll find a radio and vector 'em in."

Another huge explosion interrupted them, sending long, jagged cracks down the walls and across the floors. Computer monitors shook; some fell off the desks. "We'd better get that message out quick!" Keller shouted, pointing at the wall. The cracks were growing larger, and water had begun to pour in.

* * *

The tremors sent shock waves through Megatron's shackles. Ever so slowly, a piece of his cryo-ice chipped off. Then another. Then another. Water gushed over his head, melting the ice even faster. The robot's eyes began to open. He moved a finger, and then an arm. All at once, Megatron broke loose, the remaining ice crumbling off him in huge shards. He ripped off the tubes that connected him to the monitors and gauges, and stepped into the deserted center of the room.

He was *free*. Finally. And he could sense the others were close by.

Wasting no time, he began to morph into an evil-looking, black, hypersonic alien jet. It looked like nothing this world had ever created. Megatron fired up his turbines and launched toward the dam's massive tunnel exit, a plume of smoke streaming behind him.

am and Mikaela led Bumblebee to the Allspark. They heard the crashes of what probably was World War III above them. "Whatever you're gonna do, big guy, do it fast!" Sam said.

Slowly, the Allspark moved toward Bumblebee, as if magnetized. Tendrils of energy arced between the Allspark and Bumblebee's hands. Sam caught his breath. It was as if they were talking to each other.

The Allspark's sides began to fold in. Then again. It continued to fold in on itself, becoming exponentially smaller, until it was the size of a football. When Sam and Mikaela looked at Bumblebee again, he had transformed into the Camaro. His backseat door swung open, and the Allspark floated inside. A seatbelt lashed across it, strapping it in.

Sam and Mikaela dashed into the car just as the silo's walls started to crumble. Bumblebee peeled out through the long tunnel out of the dam to safety.

* * *

As the dam crumbled, a sleek jet burst out of the rubble and sliced into the sky. It landed on top of the Hoover Dam and began to transform . . . into Megatron.

Starscream, the fighter jet, landed to meet him. So did Brawl, Bonecrusher, Barricade, and Frenzy, all raring to go after their long journeys here.

"Lord Megatron," Starscream said. "We are ready to transform the machines."

"Good," Megatron boomed.

But something felt wrong. Megatron could sense the Allspark was no longer close. He narrowed his eyes and scanned the desert highway until he saw a yellow Camaro, speeding away. Two kids sat in the front seat . . . and there was the Allspark, strapped in the back.

Megatron glowered at Starscream. "Don't let them get away."

The Decepticons took off. Bonecrusher gnashed his giant mandibles and threw the other cars on the highway aside. Barricade turned on his police lights, clearing a path through the remaining traffic. When he got closer to the Camaro, he realized that the Search and Rescue vehicle, pickup, sports car, and eighteen-wheeler driving next to Bumblebee weren't ordinary vehicles, but Autobot bodyguards: Ratchet, Ironhide, Jazz . . . and Optimus Prime.

At one hundred miles per hour, Bonecrusher transformed from mine-sweeping vehicle to robot, slamming a steel foot on the highway, ripping up asphalt, and causing traffic behind him to veer fearfully to the shoulder. He pounced on Optimus, who instantly transformed as well. The robots collided, rolling off the freeway overpass and crashing to the level below. Optimus rose and laser-pulsed Bonecrusher, sending him flailing into a cement river basin.

Barricade transformed and joined the battle, slamming his fist into Optimus's back. Optimus reared up, somersaulted midair, and kicked Barricade in the chest. Barricade flew into the basin on top of Bonecrusher. Both Decepticons groaned, unable to stand. Optimus planted his foot on them, holding them down, relieved that this fight had been relatively easy. He knew, though, this was just the start.

"I don't know if this is going to work!" Glen cried. He, Maggie, Keller, and Simmons soldered two pieces of Hoover Dam radio equipment together, hoping to make something that could transmit Morse code.

Slam! Everyone froze. Something banged at the door. *Slam! Slam!* Dents began to form in the door's superstrong steel. Everyone exchanged nervous glances. *An alien?*

The monster kept pounding. Maggie shoved a giant cabinet against the doors, but a long, steel head poked through the crack. He gnashed his teeth and looked carefully at the three of them.

Frenzy.

The skinny monster spewed giant steel discs from his chest. The discs shot through the room and embedded into the far wall. "Get down!" Keller shouted.

More discs came flying. Maggie ducked under a desk; Simmons cowered behind the radio equipment. The discs tore through the overhead lamps, sending shards of filaments raining down on the carpet. A monitor smashed to pieces.

"I got it to work!" Glen called from the machine. "We're transmitting!"

Keller ran over to Glen. "Transmit exactly what I say: 'This is Defense Secretary Keller, get me NORTHCOM commander, authenticate emergency action Blackbird one-one-nine-five Alpha, over!"

"Okay, okay," Glen said.

Suddenly, the double doors buckled and the cabinet went flying. In came the scrawny monster. He scampered to the center of the room, hunched down, and hissed.

"What do we do?" Simmons whispered.

Maggie noticed a weapons box in the corner. She ran to it and pulled out a shotgun. The beast skittered around the room, hissing and spitting. He sent out another round of discs, breaking two more monitors and decimating a printer.

Maggie stepped forward, her hands shaking. She aimed right for the creature, shut her eyes, and *bang!*

The gun kicked back in her hands. The robot shrieked in pain.

"They responded!" Glen cried from the radio.

"Call in the strike!" Keller shouted. "Fast!"

"All right!" Glen transmitted furiously. "This killer robot's a little distracting, though!"

Frenzy struggled to his feet. Maggie shot again, but missed. She tried once more, but nothing came out. The gun was empty. The beast lunged and pinned her to the ground, wrapping his fingers around her throat.

"Not so fast." Keller strained to hold a heavy fax machine over Frenzy's narrow head. He dropped it, and the machine crashed to the ground, landing squarely on the monster. With a squeal, Frenzy released his grip on Maggie and went limp.

Maggie and Keller stood back, catching their breath. Then, they both turned to Glen and said at exactly the same time, "Did you get the message out?"

Glen slumped at the console. "Yes."

Bumblebee had sped through the dusty desert, the Allspark safely strapped into his backseat. He had now arrived in the closest city. Sam and Mikaela stepped out of the car, and the other Autobots rolled up beside them. Lennox and Epps, who had followed in artillery buggies, joined them, too. They all looked around, trying to figure out their next move.

Lennox eyed a pawnshop and ducked in. A large, grumpy-faced woman in a muumuu glared at him.

"I need that shortwave radio," Lennox said to her, pointing behind the counter. It was the perfect radio to call the air force planes from the air after Maggie, Keller, and the others sent the Morse code signal. If they could even send the signal . . .

The pawnshop owner scowled. "Are you payin' cash?"

Lennox ran his hands over his eyes. Of course

he didn't have any cash. He'd been on a Middle Eastern base for months. And now he was fighting aliens. "Look, you can have my watch," he argued desperately, sliding it off his wrist. "It's air force issue, tells perfect time, you can scuba-dive to thirty meters . . ."

The woman pointed to herself. "Do I look like I'm going to be scuba diving to you?" But she rolled her eyes and took the radio from the shelf.

Lennox ran out into the street and slid a battery into the radio's back. "CQ, CQ, WR2, GFO!" he shouted into the microphone. "Come back, do you copy?"

The only response was static. Sam, Mikaela, and the Autobots looked at them, worried. When they saw the F-22 fighter plane scream above them, everyone whooped with joy. "Oh, baby!" Lennox cried. "The air force has arrived! CQ, CQ, WR2, GFO. We see you! You're headed to our position!"

Still more static, but the jet kept coming. Sensing something was wrong, the Autobots transformed. And at that very minute, the jet dropped through the buildings, flew straight toward them, and started to fire!

"*Mooooove!*" Lennox shouted.

As the jet passed over them, everyone saw the logo on the plane's underbelly. The logo wasn't the air force's majestic wings, but the Decepticons' mask.

Starscream.

Bumblebee and Ironhide flipped over an old truck to shield the humans from Starscream's attack. The evil plane's missile shot straight for them, instantly turning the ground into a bonfire and sending the Autobots sliding backward. When the smoke cleared, they could see a small, silver object soaring through the air. *The Allspark!*

The Allspark bounced to Earth, radiating a shock wave from its core. The wave filtered out to an SUV two streets away. In seconds, every electronic device inside the car came alive. The driver and passenger ran screaming into the street.

Lennox grasped the CB radio. "We're under heavy fire!" he called. "Does anyone copy?"

Finally, a staticky voice answered. "Yes . . . army Black Hawk . . . inbound . . . lay down your . . . coordinates." Lennox quickly gave the Black Hawk pilot their location. "Copy that," the pilot said.

"ETA . . . two minutes."

Meanwhile, Blackout the chopper landed on a building roof and transformed. Soldiers ran to him and began shooting. The ground began to tremble. They turned and saw Brawl the Decepticon tank rolling toward them, flattening everything in his path. The cannon turret on Brawl's arm slowly pivoted toward Sam and Mikaela. Sam grabbed Mikaela's hand and looked around. There was nowhere for them to hide.

A giant foot landed next to them. Jazz! The Autobot leaped onto Brawl, knocking him backward. Brawl then staggered forward, but Jazz spin-kicked him into a building. Brick crumbled everywhere. Ratchet and Ironhide joined the fight, sledgehammering Brawl with all they had. Their lasers pierced deep into Brawl's steel flesh, and suddenly, Brawl began to melt, transforming into a molten puddle.

Jazz stepped back, satisfied—suddenly, a supernova of fire ripped him open from behind. He flew into the air and fell lifelessly to the ground. Out of the shadows stepped Megatron.

Sam gasped. Megatron was free?

Megatron's firepower had blasted Jazz's whole middle away, revealing his tangled, mechanical insides—including his Spark, which was throbbing away in his chest. Megatron hovered over Jazz hungrily. Ratchet flung himself onto Megatron's back, but Megatron shook him off, as if Ratchet were a mere fly. Then, Megatron reached into Jazz's chest and ripped out his Spark, efficiently and confidently.

"No!" Ironhide screamed. Jazz crumpled to the ground.

They heard a rumbling from behind. A massive truck headed right for the battle. Mid-stride, the truck began to get taller and taller . . . forming legs, then arms, then a head. *Optimus.*

Megatron narrowed his eyes, transformed into a jet, and flew straight into Optimus, catching him by the shoulder and pulling him high into the air. He misjudged the height of an oncoming billboard, however, and smashed right through it. Both the robot and the plane crashed to earth. They quickly pushed themselves back up and stared each other down.

"Megatron," Optimus boomed.

"Optimus," Megatron answered. "You still make allies of the weak."

"Where you see weakness, I see strength," Optimus responded.

"So be it, brother," Megatron hissed. "Our war begins again here. On Earth."

They collided. Optimus lasered Megatron's chest. Megatron's arms became two dozen firing turrets. They launched all at once, sending Optimus flying backward an entire city block. He landed with a boom that shook the whole street. Optimus groaned . . . and seemed to surrender.

Megatron turned away. He puffed up his chest, as if to say, *Ha. That was easy.*

* * *

Starscream's blast had knocked Sam out. He woke up next to some garbage cans and looked around. *The Allspark! Where is it?* He spied it lying, unprotected, near a fire hydrant, and he sprinted toward it. Bumblebee got there first—only he wasn't walking. His torso was a mass of twisted wires and steel; Starscream's blast had severed his legs cleanly off.

"Bumblebee!" Sam cried.

Bumblebee pulled the Allspark out from behind the fire hydrant and handed it to Sam. *Go,* his pleading eyes seemed to say. *Get this out of here.*

"No way!" Sam whimpered, panicked. "I'm not leaving you!"

Go, Bumblebee's eyes begged.

A black shadow loomed overhead. They heard the *thump-thump* of rotor blades. A swarm of army Black Hawks blurred past. "Thank goodness," Sam whispered.

"Kid!" Lennox came running over to Sam. "Here's a flare! Get to the highest rooftop you can find, signal the chopper, and *get out of here!* We'll cover for you!"

Sam widened his eyes. The *roof?* It was completely open! Decepticons would pummel him! "But, what am I supposed to . . ." He started to quake with fear.

Lennox put his face close to Sam's. "It's time to see what you're made of, soldier! You gotta get that Allspark far outta the city—as far as you can— or a lot of people are going to die!"

Sam protested, but Lennox pushed him toward the building. Sam turned around and glanced at

Bumblebee, but Bumblebee urged him on. Sam took a few terrified steps . . . and then Blackout's giant foot slammed down inches away. Sam screamed.

Blackout reached out for the Allspark. Sam shut his eyes. *I can't do this,* he thought. *I can't save the world. I'm just a scrawny kid who didn't even make the football team.*

Then, Lennox's words rang out in his head. *Time to see what you're made of, soldier!* He thought of Optimus and Bumblebee. Of Jazz, and of how Megatron tore Jazz's Spark from his chest.

He couldn't let the Decepticons win.

Sam stood up, tucked the Allspark under his arm, and darted for the nearby building. He swerved right and left, between the Decepticons' legs, into alleys, and through narrow passageways where the huge robots couldn't go. Finally, he came to the building's entrance, found the stairwell, and leaped up the stairs three at a time.

"Army Black Hawks, request immediate evacuation for civilian boy with cargo," said Epps into the radio. "He's headed to the rooftop of the highest structure."

The stairs beneath Sam shook. Sam grasped the railing, trying to keep his footing, and then he looked down. The stairwell beneath him had crumbled away! Sam scurried up the remaining stairs—he could see the door to the roof just ahead.

And then, a giant steel head crashed through the wall. Sam cowered back. It was *Megatron*!

18

Sam scrambled through the door to the roof, desperately trying to escape Megatron. He scanned the sky and saw the army chopper off in the distance. "Here I am!" he cried, setting off the flare.

The chopper flew over and signaled for Sam to come to the building's edge. An army commando dangled out the chopper's door. "Take my hand, kid!"

Suddenly, Starscream whipped through the sky, lasers blazing. Everything went white and smoky. Sam somersaulted midair, landing painfully on his stomach, the Allspark still wrapped in his arms. Starscream fired again, hitting the chopper's propeller. It rapidly spiraled downward.

At the same time, Megatron smashed his head through the concrete roof. He pulled himself through and spied Sam. "Give me the Allspark, boy!" he roared. "You aren't strong enough to defy me!"

"No!" Sam cried, scrambling for the edge of the building. *Maybe there will be another helicopter,* he thought. *Maybe someone will still save me.*

"I see fear in your eyes," Megatron taunted. "Give it to me, and I'll let you go. Don't, and you'll die."

Sam hiked the Allspark higher in his arms. "I am never giving it to you."

"Fine!" Flames shot out of Megatron's arms, blowing out the rooftop beneath him. Sam toppled over the edge.

Optimus, still weakened from his battle with Megatron, saw Sam fall. He sprang up creakily and, with all of his might, lunged toward Sam's building. He stuck out his palm and caught Sam just before he hit the pavement. *Slap!* Sam rolled into his palm. He gave Optimus a grateful smile and then pointed to the Allspark, wedged under his arm.

Optimus gasped. "You would give your own life to protect the Allspark?"

"No sacrifice, no victory," Sam croaked. It was something his father always said. He'd never understood it . . . until right now.

* * *

Meanwhile, Bumblebee had collapsed on the sidewalk. Mikaela and a few soldiers rolled his severed legs to him, and slowly, the legs began to fuse back into his body. After a few minutes, nearly half of the legs had regenerated. Mikaela tried to help Bumblebee to stand, but he was too weak.

Mikaela looked around and had an idea. She ran to a tow truck across the street, hot-wired it to life, and jerked it into reverse until she could hook Bumblebee's chassis to its chains. She hit the lever, and the chains pulled Bumblebee up . . . but he still couldn't stand. Frustrated, Mikaela got out.

Stomp . . . stomp . . .

Mikaela swiveled around and screamed. Bonecrusher, the mine-clearing vehicle, stormed straight toward them. Before she could take cover, Bonecrusher fired, knocking Mikaela off her feet into the tow truck. When she came to, the Decepticon stood almost on top of her. Bumblebee whimpered, helpless.

"It's okay," Mikaela reassured him, getting another idea. She climbed onto Bumblebee's chest and lifted his arm. "Okay. I'll aim, you shoot."

Bumblebee's arm transformed into a laser turret.

"Now!" Mikaela cried, and a molten stream of fire burst forth. Asphalt exploded just to the left of Bonecrusher, but the Decepticon was unhurt. Mikaela aimed again. *Blam!* This time the shot landed just to their right.

"Last one," Mikaela said through her teeth. Bonecrusher, just feet away, laughed sinisterly. "We've got to get it perfect." Mikaela closed her eyes and shot. *Blam!* It caught Bonecrusher right in his grill. The vehicle flipped over their heads, hitting the ground hard and splintering into a million alien pieces.

Mikaela patted Bumblebee's arm. "Nice shot."

* * *

Optimus put Sam down on the ground when, suddenly, they felt a presence behind them. *Megatron.* He transformed quickly from a jet into a robot and stomped toward them. Sam cowered between Optimus's mighty legs.

"It's mine!" Megatron boomed. "The Allspark is mine!"

Blackout and Starscream surrounded Optimus, trying to distract him from Sam. They hit Optimus with beam after beam of firepower, and Optimus thrashed and groaned. Starscream got in a punch to Optimus's stomach, and Optimus sank to his knees. The two Decepticons surrounded him, pummeling his head. It looked like the end.

Suddenly, air force jets screamed low, dropping the high-heat laser rounds on Blackout and Starscream. *Bull's-eye!* A white-hot laser seared through Blackout, blowing his armor wide open. Lennox jumped onto a nearby abandoned motorcycle, slid the bike under the robot's legs, and fired with his own high-heat laser launcher. The rounds tore into Blackout's chest, stomach, limbs . . . everywhere. The Decepticon screamed and began to disintegrate.

Seeing his opportunity, Optimus pushed himself up and smacked Starscream across the jaw. Starscream backed away, squared his shoulders, and charged. Optimus raised his leg and gave him a powerful, penetrating roundhouse kick, sending Starscream into a row of cars. Optimus retreated, victorious . . . but then he remembered. *Sam! The Allspark!*

He spied Sam fifty yards away, the Allspark tucked under his arm, sprinting with everything he had. Megatron was gaining on him!

"It's mine!" Megatron roared, each of his footfalls making craters in the pavement. "The Allspark is mine!" Military jets streaked past him, dropping missiles, but nothing could slow him down.

Optimus staggered after them, but it was too late: Sam had run blindly down a dead-end alley. Sam ran the whole way to the end before realizing his mistake. He turned around, quivering. Megatron, just large enough to fit through the passageway, barreled toward him.

"Give me the Allspark," Megatron growled, his eyes glowing red.

Sam's heart pounded. He hugged the Allspark to his chest.

"No."

Optimus ran to edge of the alley. He was too large to fit through. "Sam! Use the Allspark!"

"Huh?" Sam stared at the Allspark. "What do you mean?"

"Aim for his Spark!"

Megatron picked up Sam by his collar, lifting him into the air. Sam thrashed wildly. The Allspark felt slippery in his hands. Megatron's fingers squeezed his neck. Sam swore he could feel his own bones breaking.

"Aim for his Spark! Do it now!" Optimus roared.

What did Optimus mean "use the Allspark"? What was he supposed to do? Sam stared at the bullet wounds in Megatron's armor and at a raw section of his arm and his chest. Deep inside, Sam could see Megatron's Spark, throbbing away. And then, suddenly, he got it. He was supposed to use the Allspark as a weapon.

Here goes nothing, Sam thought, and jammed the Allspark into Megatron's chest.

Megatron instantly dropped Sam and started to wail. The Allspark shuddered. Huge cords of electricity spiraled from it, turning Megatron's armor from silver to orange to blue to a charred black.

Megatron tried to pry the Allspark from his chest, but it wouldn't budge. The Allspark snapped and vibrated, and Megatron's Spark sizzled faster and faster. And then, abruptly, his Spark exploded, sending out a pulse of energy so strong, it thrust Sam up against the wall. Megatron arched his back in a final, labored struggle, and then he went limp.

Starscream, sprawled atop the line of cars, quickly realized what had happened. As the one remaining Decepticon, he transformed . . . and soared higher into the sky. Perhaps even leaving the planet . . . for good.

After that, there was a long silence.

* * *

The smoke began to clear. Mikaela helped Bumblebee limp toward the others. They joined Sam, Lennox, Optimus, and the other Autobots in a circle around the fallen Megatron.

Sam stared at the Allspark in Megatron's chest. It had shriveled and was now a dull gray, and looked like nothing more than a rock. Sam looked at Optimus. "But your planet! Without the Allspark, you're the last of your kind."

"We will survive." Optimus glanced at Jazz's twisted, lifeless corpse. "For those that did not."

Then Mikaela gasped and pointed at Megatron. "Look at his eyes!" The last glazed glow in his eyes had dwindled out.

"You left me no choice, brother." Optimus sighed. "You left me no choice."

AIRCRAFT CARRIER, THE LAURENTIAN ABYSS

On Monday morning, Maggie and Keller stood at the bow of an aircraft carrier as pulleys dragged something across the flight deck. Something big, bigger than any man. Something that had to be kept a dark secret.

They took one last look at Megatron. His eyes were dull and lifeless, the Allspark had shriveled to a tiny pea-shaped indentation in his chest, and they'd harnessed a bolt-studded nuclear device to his waist. The world would never know of his existence, thanks to the satellite blackouts during the attack. To maintain absolute secrecy, Sector Seven had disbanded as well. All those who did know swore never to tell.

The technicians shoved Megatron overboard. The Decepticon sank fast, the blinding detonator light on his chest growing dim. "Three, two, one," the technician said, but the only indication of the explosion was a muffled boom. Bubbles burbled to the surface.

Maggie turned to Keller. "The other Decepticons . . . they're gone, too, right?"

"Mm-hmm," Keller said. They had gone in for reconnaissance and cleanup just hours after the attack, hauling away the others' mangled bodies.

"But . . ." Maggie paused. "What about the ones helping us—the Autobots? What happened to them?"

Keller sighed. Four of the Autobots had survived the attack. Shortly after the battle, however, all of them—including the one who had perished—had vanished.

Maggie shifted uneasily. Keller's silence had confirmed what she suspected. *They're still here,* she thought. *But . . . where?*

TRANQUILITY HIGH, TRANQUILITY, U.S.A.

Sam walked through the halls to his next class. Suddenly, he saw Mikaela ahead of him. She stood against her locker, looking right at him and smiling. Sam's heart beat very fast. Then he noticed that Trent DeMarco stood a few steps ahead of him.

Well, Sam thought, *looks like things are back to normal, after all.*

Mikaela came closer and closer. Trent stepped in her path, but she skirted around him . . . and walked right up to Sam.

"Hey, Sam," she said.

"Hey," he said back.

"Good weekend?" she asked.

Before Sam could answer, she kissed him, long and hard, right on his lips. In front of Trent. In front of everyone.

Sam glanced out the window to the student lot, where he'd parked his new Camaro GTO. More than anything, he wanted to run out and tell Bumblebee what had just happened. But then . . . that might be weird. Cool kids, after all, didn't talk to their cars.

RURAL FARMHOUSE, OKLAHOMA

A woman stepped out onto her porch. She held her baby in her arms. When she saw the pickup far down the road coming toward them, she smiled excitedly. Daddy was home.

The truck rolled right into their driveway, and Lennox stepped out. He ran up to his wife and gave her a huge hug, and then he stepped back and took his baby girl into his arms for the first time.

Optimus, perched atop a mountain not far away, watched all of this. He locked eyes with Lennox's pickup, Ironhide, and smiled.

"I am Optimus Prime," he said in his ancient, alien language. "I send this message to all surviving Autobots taking refuge among the stars. You are not alone. It is safe here. We are waiting."

He stared up at the clear, blue sky. Optimus felt comforted to think of his signal, rising higher and higher into the sky, traveling faster than the speed of light. Perhaps it was reaching one of the other Autobots right now, someone far away, possibly frightened, afraid that they no longer had a home.

But they did have a home. Earth. It was a strange home, but it was something. Its people had a great capacity for courage and strength. Much like the Autobots, there was more to earthlings than met the eye.

Optimus stared at the sky for a long time. He hoped someone would receive his signal. He hoped someone would answer.